**His eyes were cold and dark
as graveyard clay...**

Bannerman growled deep in his throat. "The man I'm waiting for is said to drop by often enough after work. His name is Custis Long. Some calls him Longarm. I mean to make his name *mud,* afore sundown!"

Emma Gould gasped incredulously and said, "Save your money, mister. For, in the first damn place, Longarm won't be coming through yon door in the foreseeable future. And, in the second place, they'll need what's in your pockets to bury you proper, once you *do* meet up with him!"

Bannerman shifted his weight in the chair ominously as he said, half to himself, "I've had five years in prison to heal my shooting arm good and think bad thoughts about the son of a bitch. So this time things figures to go my way, see?"

**TABOR EVANS**

# LONGARM

## IN THE BITTERROOTS

A JOVE BOOK

LONGARM IN THE BITTERROOTS

A Jove Book/published by arrangement with
the author

PRINTING HISTORY
Jove edition/October 1985

ISBN: 0-515-08367-4

Jove books are published by The Berkley Publishing Group,
200 Madison Avenue, New York, N.Y. 10016. The words
"A JOVE BOOK" and the "J" with sunburst are trademarks
belonging to Jove Publications, Inc.

PRINTED IN THE UNITED STATES OF AMERICA

# Chapter 1

The Professor was paid to do more than play piano in a house of ill repute. So when he saw trouble brooding in the far corner of the downstairs parlor, nursing its drink and not even looking up when French Alice passed by naked as a jay on her way to the bar to wash her sassy mouth out with sloe gin after kissing her last customer adios, albeit not on the mouth, the Professor let go the ivories long enough to pass the word to Madam Emma. The handsome but hard-faced Emma Gould took one look at the stranger from between the red velvet drapes across her office door near the piano and said, "You done right to tell me, Professor. For if there's one thing that moody gent ain't looking for, it's our usual services!"

"Want me to round up Spike and Pee-Wee, Madam Emma?"

"Not yet. The Denver police frown on bouncing tedious customers Dodge City style. I'd best have a motherly talk with the son of a bitch first."

1

The broodsome stranger in the corner didn't look up as Emma Gould approached as sedately as even a fully dressed gal could in such unseemly surroundings. For though Madam Emma herself was too sedate or mayhaps too old to cater personally to the customers, it was an established fact that she ran the biggest, meanest whorehouse in Denver, if not the entire state of Colorado.

By the time she'd pulled a bentwood chair from the wall and sat down beside him, Madam Emma had sized the stranger up as a no longer young and never too good-looking gent, dressed cow, but too pale of face and hands to have worked with cows or anything else outdoors in recent memory. His blue denim shirt and pants looked new. His hat, boots, and buscadero gun rig looked worn and faded as him. Madam Emma pasted an insincere smile across her painted face and said, "I hope you have a permit for that old thumb-buster you're packing, mister. For there's a Denver City ordinance against the display of such hardware on the streets, of late. Denver's gotten awfully sissy since they put in them new street lamps. I'm called Madam Emma, by the way."

The middle-aged stranger didn't look at her as he replied, "I know. My handle is Bannerman. I ain't here to cause trouble for you or yourn, Madam Emma. So why can't you jest let me be? Your barkeep can tell you I paid for this fool drink, and I ain't looking to git laid, see?"

Emma Gould followed his morose gaze and nodded thoughtfully. "I can see you're covering the front door from here, and if that don't spell trouble for me and mine I don't know what else to call it," she said. "I only pay the precinct captain to ignore petty indiscretions, mister. A gunfight in my front parlor would upset the neighbors awful, that Persian rug would cost a bundle to clean, and

2

the copper badges would charge even more to write the whole thing up polite."

Bannerman reached for his wallet, took out a hundred dollars in silver certificates, and held them out to the whore, growling, "Here. The police won't want more'n twenty apiece, lemon juice is good for bloodstains, and there ain't a precinct captain west of the Big Muddy who can't be bought for fifty."

"That still don't leave me much of a profit. No offense."

For the first time Bannerman looked her full in the face and the hard-boiled whore blanched in mortal fear as their eyes locked. Bannerman's eyes were cold and dark as graveyard clay and his voice rasped like the hinges of a tomb as he replied, "A hundred is all I have to spare. I know it ain't much, but consider how much more expensive it could get if you tried to throw me out. You'd best set somewheres else, Madam Emma. You ain't in my line of fire, but the man I'm waiting for may get off a round or two in this general direction as he goes down."

Emma Gould was pretty scared by now, but she'd never gotten to the top of her tough profession by being a sissy. So she held her ground, or at least her seat, and insisted, "See here, I run a respectable establishment, and I expect my customers to conduct themselves the same. The house rules say you can drink yourself unconscious, screw yourself silly, or even study French, if you're willing to pay extra. But gunplay ain't allowed on or about these here premises."

Bannerman didn't answer. He turned his cold, deadly eyes on the front door again. His Colt .45 Conversion was slung cross-draw. Emma had learned in her younger days in Dodge that a seated man could draw tolerable,

3

cross-draw. She licked her lips. "Well, since you won't listen to reason, I'd best clear the parlor and roll up the rug," she said. "But would you mind telling me just who you're waiting here for? Any man dumb enough to cross anyone serious as you no doubt has it coming. But I'm sort of distressed to hear it's one of our regular customers. For, like I said, I try to run an orderly establishment, and I can tell you true we don't serve many noted gun-slicks here!"

Bannerman growled deep in his throat. "The man I'm waiting for is said to drop by often enough after work. His name is Custis Long. Some calls him Longarm. I mean to make his name *mud*, afore sundown!"

Emma Gould gasped incredulously and said, "They told you you'd be likely to meet Longarm *here*, and, worse yet, you mean to go up agin him with a single-action hog-leg? Save your money, mister. For, in the first damn place, Longarm won't be coming through yon door in the foreseeable future. And, in the second place, they'll need what's in your pockets to bury you proper, once you *do* meet up with him!"

Bannerman shrugged. "Don't really matter all that much which of us gets buried, as long as I gets my chance, at last, to have it out fair and square with the rascal. Last time we met I'd been winged already in the right shoulder and, aside from that, he had the drop on me afore he announced his presence, from ahint me." Bannerman shifted his weight in the chair ominously as he added, half to himself, "I've had five years in prison to heal my shooting arm good and think bad thoughts about the son of a bitch. So this time things figures to go more my way, see?"

"I see someone's fed you a bucket of snipe feathers." Madam Emma smiled, adding, "It's true Deputy U.S.

4

Marshal Custis Long has done me and mine a favor or two in the past and been repaid in kind, albeit not in the manner gossip might have it. I've *offered* to repay him in a more personal way, cuss his romantic nature. For to tell the truth I'd surely like to know if that tall rascal is as tall as some gals say he is in bed. But our only relationship has been that betwixt a lawman and a . . . well, let's say a lady who likes to stay on the good side of the law, within reason."

Bannerman didn't answer. He'd about finished his drink by now and if it had any mellowing effect on him, it didn't show. Madam Emma insisted, "He ain't coming, damn it. I knows for a fact he's been on court duty all week and he never comes here unless it's to ask questions, say about a new big spender in town shortly after a holdup Uncle Sam might have a personal interest in. Longarm's a federal deputy. He takes no personal interest in local lawbreaking. That's one reason we get along so well, see?"

She smiled sheepishly. "Though he did warn me one time about a pure Injun gal I had working the cribs upstairs. He said he meant to take her back to her folk on the reservation and that my own hired guns could stand aside or not, as they seen fit. As you can no doubt guess, we let him take the fool squaw peaceably."

Bannerman frowned thoughtfully and said, "All right, if he don't really come by here after he gets off duty at the federal building, where *do* he go for relaxation?"

Emma Gould knew, of course, but she said she had no idea. She got to her feet. "It's been nice talking to you, mister," she said. "But now that anyone can see you're on a fool's errand, we'll just leave the rug where it is and, if you'd like another drink, it's on the house. You just stay as long as you like, hear?"

5

Bannerman didn't answer. He didn't think he had to. Madam Emma made a gracious round of the parlor, nodding and making small talk to her few early and less truculent customers. Then, as soon as she could do so without it seeming obvious, she ducked out, grabbed a colored maid in the hall, and said, "Willie, put your street duds on, pronto. Then make tracks to the Black Cat and, if he ain't there, try Henry's, over by the Burlington Yards."

The maid nodded. "Yes'm. But who is I lookin' fo' and how come?" she asked.

"Longarm," Emma Gould said. "You're to call him Deputy Long, you sassy Negra. Tell him Logan Bannerman is gunning for him, and don't ask me who in thunder Logan Bannerman is! All I know is that Longarm must have arrested him one time and that he's out again and on the prod. So *move* it, Willie!"

The maid did, and she might have found Longarm in time had he been at either of the watering places Emma Gould knew he frequented. But there were more than two such establishments in the city of Denver and, as Logan Bannerman was finding out the hard way, Longarm was not a creature of habit. A man in his line of work couldn't afford to be. So that should have been the end of the matter and would have been, had it not been for a false-hearted woman.

Madam Emma was back in her office again, counting all her money, when Blue Tooth Rowena plunked her bare rump down on the chair the madam had vacated and said, "I couldn't help but overhear, dear."

Bannerman kept staring at the front door, despite the state of undress Blue Tooth Rowena was in. But he must have noted the sassy little redhead was there, and tolerable to look at, for he growled, "Another time, Red.

You ain't bad, but I'm here in search of other pleasures."

"I know," she said, "but Old Emma tolt you true. Ain't neither of us fixing to see Longarm here tonight. But what would it be worth to you if I *could* steer you to the proper time and place?"

Bannerman turned in his seat to stare her way, cold as a banker's heart, and Blue Tooth Rowena added, "He won't be back at the Black Cat this evening because he had a fuss with a barmaid there. He won't be at Henry's because a certain fancy widow woman up to Sherman Avenue knows he hangs out there and *she's* mad at him, too."

"That sounds like the Longarm we all knows and loves, Red. So tell me, where *might* he be drinking this evening?"

The whore shook her red head and said, "Not so fast, mister. I gives it three ways for two dollars. But I don't give nothing away for *free*, if you follows my drift."

Bannerman grimaced. "I never asks a lady to do nothing for nothing. But, no offense, I paid to learn he'd be coming here this evening and, as you can plainly see, I got took. So, whilst I values such information as you may have for sale to the tune of one hundred U. S. dollars, you'll have to wait for it till after, see?"

Blue Tooth Rowena shook her head again. "Sorry, pard, I don't extend credit to gents I don't know and, if I did, I'd still be a fool to accept an I.O.U. from a man going up agin *Longarm!* You can pay in advance, or find him your ownself."

She started to rise, but Bannerman's big left paw shot out quick as a diamondback and pulled her down in his lap. "You ain't going nowheres till you tell me true, Red! I've waited five whole years to pay that bastard back and, do you cross me, I'll just have to bust your pretty neck, hear?"

Blue Tooth Rowena was only too aware that the few people watching found nothing unusual in the sight of a nearly naked whore seated in a customer's lap. From the funny way he was breathing she could tell he was either fixing to have an orgasm or an awesome fit of temper. So she tried to relax in his iron grip as she soothed, "Hey, don't bruise my merchandise, handsome! I don't like the son of a bitch neither, see?"

"Never mind why. I reckon I knows. Just tell me where he's *at!*"

"Could you mayhaps give me half now and the rest when through, lover man?"

"I'll give you twenty and no more afore I leave. I'll give you the rest when I come back. For I'm coming back, whether you're lying to me or not, and, if you are, I'll kill you. I've been waiting *five years,* Red, and you've no idea how much hate a man can store up in that time, just a-staring at his cell bars and a-counting the days!"

Blue Tooth Rowena nodded soberly and said, "I'm good at holding grudges, too, and it's only been a couple of weeks since Longarm shamed me by turning down a well-intended offer with a knowing laugh."

She hesitated, glanced about to make sure she wasn't being overheard, then murmured, "There's a saloon calt the Parthenon, near the federal building. Longarm's been drinking there after work this week because it's close to the courtroom he's been stuck in all day and because they got a new barmaid calt Kitty working at the Parthenon."

Bannerman nodded, let go the whore, and rose a good six feet and a half as he got out his wallet again and paid off before leaving, not saying another word. As Blue Tooth Rowena put the folded bill away under a frilly garter, another whore asked, "Whoo-eee! What on earth did he order for that *kind* of money, Rowena, dear?"

Blue Tooth Rowena looked away and said, "It was too dirty to talk about in mixed company." She didn't mean it, of course. But be it recorded most of the whores working for Emma Gould would have found the transaction too dirty indeed for them to consider. Few of them were dumb enough to offer the madam's handsome friend their wares and in truth most whores, like most women, thought Longarm a tolerably decent cuss.

As Blue Tooth Rowena went to her crib to hide her blood money away, the man she'd just betrayed wasn't bothering man, woman, or beast. For, as usual, malicious gossip had linked Longarm unfairly with the new barmaid at the Parthenon. The tall deputy was aware of the little brunette's charms, of course, since he still had eyes in his head, but like most experienced travelers, Longarm had long since learned not to start up with such gals unless they started up with him first. Working gals tended to be tediously virtuous, which was the reason they had to work in the first place, most likely, and it wasn't true the widow woman up on Sherman Avenue was mad at him this evening. Longarm meant to call on her directly, once he unwound a mite from sitting tight in federal court all afternoon. But a man of action had to stretch and move about some before he went to bed, and he knew the handsome widow woman would insist, as usual, on turning in early.

So Longarm was bellied up to the bar with his reporter friend Crawford from the *Post,* swapping lies and drinking needled beer, when Logan Bannerman parted the batwing doors behind them with his considerable bulk and called out loud and clear, "Longarm!"

Longarm had, of course, already seen him coming in.

A man in Longarm's line of work made it a habit never to drink unless he had his back to a wall or a mirror to his front. Longarm never forgot a face, either. So, though Bannerman's was older and paler, now, than it had been the last time they'd met, Longarm turned with a nod of recognition and said, "Evening, Bannerman. How come they let you out?"

Others were moving out of the line of fire now, even though the tall federal deputy seemed relaxed and friendly enough with both elbows on the bar and the grips of his double-action .44 just peeking out from under his tobacco-brown tweed coat. Bannerman stared hard at him, as if to savor the moment he'd waited so long for. But, damn it to hell, Longarm didn't even seem surprised to see him, let alone worried about it.

Longarm hadn't spent the last five years in prison, so his lean, firm-jawed face was brown enough to pass him off as an Indian, save for the heavy moustache and innocent gray eyes. Bannerman took a deep breath so his voice wouldn't crack. Then he said, "I got out early. No thanks to you. They gave me ten at hard when you arrested me five years ago. But, as you can see, it didn't stick. So here I am, and here you are, and any time you feels like filling your fist will suit me just fine, you bastard!"

Crawford of the *Post* had slid down the bar but had his notepad out as he whispered to the barkeep, "Who is that suicidal maniac, Jimbo?"

The barkeep could only whisper back, "Before my time. But they say Longarm's arrested most everyone by now. I'll be in the back if you need me."

Crawford seriously considered vaulting the bar to join him. But he was a good reporter and, worse yet, that sassy little barmaid was standing her ground, too, albeit at a discreet distance down the bar beyond Longarm. So Crawford backed into a corner booth and began taking shorthand notes as Bannerman growled, "Well?"

Longarm said, "You're out of touch with the times, old son. Since last you strode the streets of Dodge and Deadwood, they've paved the streets and buried gents like old Jim Hickock. What say you put aside the dead past and let me buy you a drink, Bannerman?"

But the man who'd come so far to kill him shook his stubborn head and insisted, "You're wrong. The past ain't dead. It's standing before me grinning that same infernal way, God damn you! What's the matter with you, anyways, Longarm? Don't you think I'm serious?"

Longarm nodded soberly. "Sure. You ain't the first ex-con who's looked me up after he got out, Bannerman. I know you took it personal when I had to take you in that time. But, what the hell, you're out now, five years earlier than you was meant to be. So now that you've done your time and paid your just debt to society, it's a time to *celebrate,* not a time to act like a mean little kid."

*"You* ain't paid your debt to *me!"* snapped Bannerman. "I tolt you when you gunned my pard and took me unfair from ahint that I meant to pay you back someday and, by the Great Horned Spoon, that day has arrived at last!"

Longarm shook his head wearily and insisted, "Bannerman, you ain't thinking this foolishness through. We're smack in the middle of a big city. Even if you won— and I wouldn't count on it—you'd just wind up before a judge again, and this time they'd hang you for sure."

"Not if I could prove it was a fair fight, damn it."

"Oh, shit, didn't they have nothing better to read in the prison library than *Ned Buntline's Wild West Mag-*

*azine*, old son? That ain't the way the law works in civilized parts like Denver. Hell, they even make *me* fill out all sorts of fool papers when I'm forced to gun a known owlhoot and, by the way, you're in violation of a local ordinance in packing that hardware on your hip inside the city limits. But, lucky for you, I ain't paid to enforce local law. So belly up by my side and let me buy you that drink while we discuss a more sensible future for you, hear?"

Bannerman looked sick, or confused, or both, as his slower wits grappled with the refusal of Longarm to play this scene the way he'd rehearsed it in his head all those prison nights. In his booth in the corner Crawford of the *Post* thought, "He's going to back down or draw. It can't go on this way much longer. The poor stupid bastard just hasn't the brains for protracted negotiations!"

Bannerman must have known that, too. His face flushed red, paled chalky, then got red again as he took a deep breath, then another. "You're just trying to mix me up, Longarm," he said. "But this time it won't work. I've come to have it out with you at last, and at last you got to fight me fair and square!"

Longarm shook his head and answered with an almost gentle smile, "Not hardly, old son. For one thing, it wouldn't *be* a fair fight, and for another, I don't like to fill out papers. Did you know they make us file our reports in triplicate these days? It's all the fault of the carbon paper trust, I'm sure. The West has sure gotten sissy since you've been away, old son. But there's nothing little gents like us can do about it. Come over here and let me buy you that drink, God damn it. Can't you see you're making all these other folk nervous with all this antiquated war talk?"

Bannerman took one step nearer before he braced his

legs in a gunfighter's stance and spat, "I never come here to talk. I come to *fight!* So what say you stand clear of that there bar and face me right. Like I said, I aim to have this reported as a fair and even fight!"

"I'm comfortable enough as I am, old son. Would it make you feel better if I turned around to lean on the bar even more so?"

"You bastard! You're trying to rattle me, ain't you?"

Longarm chuckled and replied, "Don't have to. You never was too clear a thinker, and I see soaking your head in prison hasn't done your brains much good. What line of work have you been planning on taking up now that you're a free man again, old son? There's hardly any stage lines left. On the other hand, the price of beef has risen since you was sent away, and—"

"*Draw,* you son of bitch!" croaked Bannerman, his face beet-red, and in the far corner Crawford dropped his notebook to cover his ears while, down the other way, Kitty dropped out of sight behind the bar.

But nothing happened. Bannerman had his gun hand on the grips of his own revolver. Longarm still leaned casually against the bar with both elbows braced on it, his own cross-draw rig hopelessly out of reach. So why, thought Crawford, was he still *smiling?*

It wasn't a cruel smile, or a taunting smile. It was a sort of sad and wistful smile, and it was driving Bannerman loco. The older gunslick stammered, "I'm counting to ten. Then I aim to draw. You do whatever you've a mind to, hear?"

Longarm didn't answer. Bannerman started counting. From his vantage point at a distance he could only pray was safe, Crawford had never known it could take that long to count to a hundred, let alone ten, and as Bannerman got to eight Crawford got under the table to see

13

if there could possibly be a hole in the floor.

But as Bannerman choked out, "Nine...I means it, Longarm, and, here goes, *ten!*" Longarm just suggested mildly, "Would you like to take off your boots and try for twenty?"

From under the table, Crawford heard a dull thud as something heavy hit the floor. It couldn't have been Longarm, for the reporter distinctly heard him mutter, "Aw, shit. Sorry, Miss Kitty. Forgot you was there. You can come up now."

As the barmaid peeked over the top of the bar, Crawford did the same from behind his table. They both saw Bannerman sprawled face down in the sawdust between the batwings and the bar. Longarm was moving over to him. The tall deputy dropped to one knee and felt the side of Bannerman's throat for a pulse. Then he shrugged and said, "Well, maybe it was better this way. For five years at hard hadn't done much for his *brains*, either."

Crawford's sense of duty to the *Post* overcame his natural sense of caution. He moved gingerly forward to ask Longarm, "How in the hell did you *do* that, Longarm?"

Longarm rose, removed one end of the watch chain he wore across his vest, and reattached it to the little brass derringer he'd been palming all this time in one big hand. "I didn't," he replied. "He done it to himself. I'm sorry the *Post* won't get no headlines out of this poor fool's last attempt to go out in a blaze of glory. But, like I said, the paperwork is tedious as hell, and I got me a date for later tonight."

Crawford frowned. "Hold on, now, damn it. You didn't *gun* him and I'd have surely heard if it was *suicide!* So how come he looks so dead, Longarm?"

Longarm said, "He looks dead because he *is* dead.

They let him out of Leavenworth a week ago because the prison sawbones knowed he had a bum ticker and didn't want the tax-paying public stuck with his burial on federal ground."

"He had a bad heart? You knew, all the time?"

Longarm finished putting his derringer away as he nodded and said, "Sure. That's how come I thought it wise to face him with a palmed gun, just in case the diagnosis was premature. They always tell the arresting officer when a gent he arrested is due to get out. This poor old cuss left Leavenworth muttering dark gypsy curses about me. I didn't see fit to mention this to him as he came in just now, because I didn't think it seemly to ask a dying man how much longer he had left and had I told him I'd got the wire on him, he'd have knowed I knowed how come he was out, see?"

Crawford shook his head. "I don't see at all, Longarm! How come you let him put you through all that sweatsome talk when you knew all the time he was about to drop any minute in the first place and you had him covered in the second?"

Kitty the barmaid had come around the end of the bar to join them as Crawford asked the fool question. Before Longarm could answer Kitty said, "Heavens, isn't it obvious, Mr. Crawford? Custis was too *noble* to take advantage of a sick man! He was trying to give the poor old thing a last chance to go straight!"

Longarm didn't tell her she was full of shit. It wouldn't have been polite. Crawford nodded and said, "Sure, I see it now. Bannerman knew he only had a few more days or months at the most to live. So he resolved to go out in a blaze of glory rather than go down in history as just another old outlaw, broken in health by his life of crime!"

15

Crawford moved back to the booth to get his notebook and start writing it up. A Denver copper in blue harness came through the batwings, saying, "I heard there was trouble in here and . . . Who'd you have to shoot this time, Longarm?"

Longarm said, "Didn't nobody shoot nobody, Paddy. The gent on the floor there is Logan Bannerman, a federal prisoner who just got out early because of poor health. I was just fixing to buy him a drink for old times' sake when, as you can see, his health gave out total. So what we got here is a matter for the Denver Department of Health, not the police."

He took out the watch attached to the other end of the gold-washed chain and added, "Oops, it's getting past my bedtime, folks. Crawford, here, can fill you in on the rest of it, Paddy."

He started for the door. The Denver copper said, "Hold on, Longarm. The coroner's office will surely want a statement from everyone here, no matter *how* this cuss wound up dead!"

But Longarm shook his head and replied, "I ain't a qualified M.D., and even if I was I wouldn't work as the attending physician in a case of death by natural causes. Don't try to lecture a lawman on the law, Paddy. I've sat in on more coroners' hearings than the good Lord ever intended a peaceable gent like me to. Save yourself some paperwork, too. Just call the meat wagon and let *them* decide where to haul him off to and who to tell about it. All your precinct captain will expect from you is a one-paragraph report giving the time and place a citizen dropped dead on your beat, see? The more words you put in, the more work you'll wind up making for yourself in the end, and they hardly ever promote a patrolman for pointless paperwork."

16

The copper still looked undecided. Longarm pushed through the batwings anyway. Out on the walk a crowd was gathering. Someone in it asked Longarm what was going on inside. He muttered, "Man got sick," and bulled on through. But the barmaid, Kitty, caught up with him a few doors down. When she called his name he stopped and turned, for she was prettier than anyone else in sight.

As he ticked the rim of his Stetson to her politely, Kitty said, "I have to go back to work. But I get off at midnight . . . Custis."

He smiled down at her wistfully and replied, "I know. I asked. I surely wish I could stick around to escort you home proper, Miss Kitty. But I'm on night duty, and you can see it won't be possible for a gent to sip his cider sedately in the Parthenon for a while."

Kitty nodded understandingly and said, "I'll take you up on that offer to walk me home, some other night, then. I just wanted you to know how grand I think you behaved back there just now."

"Shoot, ma'am. I don't recall behaving grand or any other way."

"You know what I mean. I confess I've asked questions about you, too, and I fear I had you down as . . . you know, a gunslick out to build a rep."

"I'm a court-appointed Deputy U. S. Marshal, Miss Kitty."

"I know. They say Wild Bill carried a badge, too. But you're not like that, Custis. You're a kind and gentle man, even if you seem ashamed to admit it. I was sure you were going to gun that poor brute in there. I could see you had that derringer covering him all the while from where I was watching from behind the bar. But you never. You tried to reason with the poor sick fool."

"Aw, mush." Longarm laughed, and then, since that

17

was hardly a polite way for a gent to dismiss a lady, even when he was in a hurry, he just hauled her in and kissed her good.

Kitty kissed back with considerable passion, shoving her firm little pelvis against him in a way they'd never have gotten away with on the street in broad daylight. When they came up for air, she murmured hopefully, "Are you sure you can't make it tonight, darling?"

He sighed and said, "Want to. Can't. When I give my word I'll be somewhere at a certain time, that's where I got to be. But unless you quit between now and tomorrow night at midnight, you'd best not make plans to walk home with any *other* gents!"

They kissed on it again to seal the bargain and she let him go. He went as fast as his stovepipe boots could carry him. But he caught hell just the same when he'd legged it up Capitol Hill to a certain brownstone house on Sherman Avenue.

The widow woman was already dressed, or rather undressed, for bed. She greeted Longarm in her darkened vestibule with, "Where have you been all this time, you rascal? You promised me you'd come straight from work, and I was about to start without you!"

He chuckled fondly, hauled her in to see if kissing her felt better or worse than kissing Kitty and, to his delight, discovered they both kissed swell, albeit each in her own different and interesting way. He said, "I'm sorry I'm late, honey. Got hung up in police matters on the way home to your loving arms. But it's over now. So what say we get out of this ridiculous vertical position?"

But the widow woman had been keeping company with Longarm longer than the barmaid at the Parthenon. So as he scooped her up to carry her upstairs, she sighed and said, "Oh, God, if you've been in another gunfight your boss, Marshal Vail, is sure to send you out of town on a field mission until it blows over, right?"

He started to reassure her, for the whole point of his having taken all that guff from the late Logan Bannerman had been to avoid just what she feared. A man had to think ahead in this business.

So he didn't tell the widow woman how hard he'd worked to assure he'd be able to give her his undivided attention through the weekend coming up. He just carried her into the bedroom, deposited her on the four-poster, and shucked his own duds to shut her up with down-home loving before she could ask more foolish questions.

It didn't work. Women were such naturally curious critters that they could ask questions in any position. So even though he had two pillows under her already ample rump and was pounding her hot and heavy, the fool gal was gasping, "Oh, you're so passionate tonight, darling! How long do you think they'll have you out in the field this time? Oh, yes, yes!"

It wouldn't have been polite to answer while they were coming together even if he'd wanted to, and he didn't. So he just kissed her hard and left it in her to keep it hard, hoping that would get her mind off official matters. But the widow woman said, "The last time Billy Vail sent you out of town to avoid your summons to a coroner's hearing I didn't see you like this for almost a month. I wish you'd learn to save your shootings for *me*, damn it! Who'd you put a round in tonight, you silly old thing?"

He got in position, grabbed a lush hip in each hand, and pulled her on like a wet glove as he chuckled and said, "As a matter of fact, I got to save all my ammunition for *you* tonight. You'll read about it in the *Post*. But old Billy may ask me to lay low for a few nights, in case

19

any of the witnesses involved require the kind of shooting I'm best at."

She giggled and arched her back as she said, "I doubt if even you could shoot better with your gun than with that lovely weapon you've got aimed at my heart so good right now."

That had been what Longarm meant. But there were times it paid a man to keep his mouth shut and just attend to the business at hand.

# Chapter 2

But the best laid plans of mice and men had a way of working out just awful. So, though Longarm reported for work at the federal building the next morning less than half an hour late and looking as innocent as he felt, he knew he was in trouble when he walked in to see the prissy clerk in the front office typing up the all-too-familiar forms he knew and loathed.

He nodded pleasantly anyway, and said, "Morning, Henry. Who's the boss sending off to God knows where by train, this time?"

The pale, pimple-faced clerk smiled back maliciously. "You, of course. You'd best go on back and get the details from the horse's mouth."

"Billy Vail ain't going to like being called a horse, Henry. But at least you called him a horse's *mouth* instead of . . . never mind. I'd best just go in and see what sort of shit he's handing me."

As usual, the pudgy older lawman seated behind the big desk glanced thoughtfully at the banjo clock on the oak-paneled wall, and as usual Longarm took a seat in the leather chair across from him and lit a cheroot in silent anticipation. Nothing that U. S. Marshal William Vail had to say during office hours was ever going to sound pleasant.

Vail had an early edition of the *Post* among the rat's nest of somewhat smaller piles of paper on his desk. He nodded curtly at Longarm and said, "I was going to give you hell for coming in late again, if only for practice. But you done right last night in the Parthenon. I'm glad it was you that poor idjet come after with a lot of wind and a bad heart. Most of my deputies would have jumped at the chance for easy target practice. How many notches do you have on your gun these days, by the way?"

Longarm shrugged. "I disremember," he said. "Never knowed a real gunfighter who went in for such fool notions, anyways. You ain't the first one to congratulate me on my noble nature, Billy. So how come that skinny son of a bitch out front is typing up travel orders for me? I wouldn't have been so patient with a no-good skunk who got his start robbing poorboxes had I thought you aimed to send me out in the field to let his corpse cool *anyways!* What does the infernal *Post* say about the way Bannerman wound up on the floor like that? I'm telling you true and official, there's no way on earth any coroner's jury can haul me before it *this* time! The asshole just fell dead at my infernal feet! I never even made a mean face at him!"

Vail nodded and said, "I know. I just read all about it. Your pal Crawford may be stretching the truth a mite for you, as he never mentions the derringer you must have been covering the ex-con with, unless you've for-

22

gotten everything I've told you. But it's obvious you knowed the rascal was sick, hoped he was as yaller as ever, and just held yourself aloof till he war-danced himself to death. As a matter of fact, and wonder of wonders, you made this department look *good* for a change! You know how often the muckraking do-gooders write us up as a mess of wild men. It was a good chance to prove we can act Christian, if only flea-bitten mad dogs will allow us to. I've already spoke to the attorney general's man down the hall. The local authorities have no call on you for this death by natural causes."

Vail pawed through the other papers on his desk, found a sheaf of yellow foolscap, and added, "It's a good thing, too. Had you been tied up with the Denver coroner's office I might not have been able to assign you to this field case."

Longarm blew smoke out both nostrils and muttered, "The asshole who said virtue was its own reward surely must have been an asshole!"

Vail had been working for the Justice Department too long to debate Longarm's observation. He scanned the first page of the complaint from the BIA, nodded to himself, and said, "I'm sending you up to the Montana Territory again. The case is federal because Montana's hardly organized for a territory, and what's been going on ain't been going on in the few parts incorporated as counties so far."

Longarm flicked tobacco ash thoughtfully on the threadbare rug to add some color. "Well, at least it's cooler up that way in high summer. But would you mind telling me what I'm supposed to do once I get there?" he asked.

Vail nodded. "The complaint is about Indians taking advantage of white folk. Indian Affairs wants it stopped."

Longarm frowned and asked, "Are you sure you're awake this early in the day, boss? No offense, but you just read that *backwards,* didn't you?"

Vail shook his head. "I thought it was a mistake the first time I read it, too. So I checked with the Bureau of Indian Affairs by wire, and they wired back more details. I know the last few times I sent you out to stare at Indians it was white crooks out to skin the redskins. But where in the U. S. Constitution does it say the white race has an exclusive franchise to diddle lesser breeds?"

Longarm shrugged and said, "I know some Indians are smarter than they let on. So what kind of a mess are the Siksika in this time?"

Vail replied, "They ain't. The Blackfoot Agency reports that, thanks to your last visit, things is tediously quiet on the High Plains of Montana. This time the trouble's with unruly Bannock over to the Bitterroot Range. The ringleader seems to be a medicine man called Weeping Snakes. So far nobody on neither side has suffered more than minor cuts and contusions, but it's only a question of time before somebody winds up prematurely bald and the army has to be called in. The BIA asked Justice to see if the dispute couldn't be settled with less noise. So guess who's it?"

Longarm protested, "Hell, Billy, I'm a lawman, not a diplomat, and even if I was, my only experience with Weeping Snakes has been at rifle range!"

"You know the rascal, Longarm?"

"Not at close range. Lucky for me, his Spencer carried a mite to the right the last time we met up. The Bannock fought on the Shoshone side when we had that war with 'em up near the South Pass a spell back. In them days, according to prisoners who had no call to lie, Weeping Snakes was a war chief, not no medicine man. I never got to discuss the matter with him personally. For some reason, every time I got within a mile of the rascal up there in the high country, he tried to blow me out of my saddle with that infernal repeating Spencer they say he took off the U.S. Cav, along with considerable hair. So if you want me to arrest Weeping Snakes for you, I'll just take along at least one troop of dragoons to back my warrant, noise or no noise!"

Vail shook his head and said, "Simmer down and pay attention to your elders, damn it. The Bannock signed the same peace treaty at the end of the Shoshone War and, aside from that, Weeping Snakes has got religion and put aside his Spencer for a Dreaming Drum. He says the spirits talk to him when he bangs his drum. Mayhaps they do. For he's surely been making mortal saps out of the local whites up along the Bitterroots. He's what you might call a tinhorn gambler or a con man if his skin was a mite paler. The more important problem is that he's got a band of at least thirty braves backing his play. The cowhands and miners up that way would know how to deal with such a flim-flam artist if he was white and riding *lonesome!* But when a man skins you at three-card monte and just stands there like a wooden Indian, with a whole mess of the same staring all about, you can accept your losses like a gent, or you can call in the army, but you ain't about to accuse nobody of *cheating* you, then and there."

Longarm laughed incredulously and said, "I thought I'd heard 'em all. But an Indian dealing three-card monte is a new one on me! I knew Weeping Snakes was a tricky old bastard and I can see how he'd think it only just to adopt the methods of his enemies. But who in thunder would be dumb enough to gamble with only semi-domesticated tribesmen in the first damn place, Billy?"

"Professional gamblers, of course," Vail said. "As you know, there's never been a federal law agin games of chance. So the tinhorn trade tends to drift to such places as the federal owned and unincorporated Bitterroots. The wandersome Bannock are a minority, even in such only half-settled country. So the faro games, monte layouts, and such are intended for the amusement of the local cowhands, miners, and more sporting sporting gals of our superior civilization. But Weeping Snakes has recently taken to riding into town, along with a nervous number of braves, to make his own modest wagers and, to the dismay of one and all, the son of a bitch seems to *win,* most every time!"

Longarm took a long, thoughtful drag on his cheroot. Then he shook his head and said, "I ain't going. We ain't got no lawful case agin that old Bannock, Billy. There's a federal law agin selling liquor to Indians. The BIA is supposed to control the sales of guns and ammo to 'em. But, thanks to your infernal habit of singling me out for cases involving Indians, I know more about BIA regulations than I ever meant to learn, and there *ain't* no law forbidding Indians to *gamble!"*

He flicked more ash on the rug as he added, "Wouldn't do any good to pass one. Next to a Chinaman, ain't nobody enjoys games of chance more'n your average Indian."

Vail shook his head and said, "You ain't been listening. I know Indians is allowed to gamble the same as anyone else, damn it. But Weeping Snakes ain't gambling. He's *winning.* Too often for the laws of chance or the regulations of the miner's vigilance committees. As to my picking you so often to deal with Indians, I have to, since you're one of my few deputies who can get along with the red rascals tolerable. I don't know why

26

Indians seem to trust you more'n the rest of us. The accounting office sure keeps giving me hell about your expense accounts and the federal prosecutors say your grasp of the rules of evidence are mighty primitive—"

Longarm cut in, "I know right from wrong, no matter how fancy it's worded. Maybe that's why Indians and me seem to agree so good on such matters. So, at the risk of repeating myself, you got no case agin Weeping Snakes if all he's done is win money off white professional gamblers! Use your fool head, Billy! What in the hell's illegal, or even *wrong*, in skinning a skinner? Don't professional gamblers take the money when *they* win?"

"They do, and when they catch someone cheating they act moody as hell about it. Weeping Snakes ain't been caught, direct, yet. But it's only a question of time before some white tinhorn figures out how he's doing it. He'd got to be doing it because nobody ever wins so consistent agin the house. The Bannock Agent's tried to show old Weeping Snakes the error of his ways, but the medicine man won't listen. He keeps insisting it's the spirits telling him how to place his bets."

Longarm asked, "How do you know they don't? What in thunder am *I* supposed to do about an Indian on a winning streak, boss? We both know I can't *arrest* him, even if his band would *let* me! If he won't listen to his own Indian agent, who has to know him and his lingo better than me, I can't think of a thing I could say to him that might make him stop. It's a fool's errand, Billy, and I got more important games of chance to investigate right here in Denver, damn it!"

Before Vail could tell him he was going anyway, the clerk came in from the front office with a sealed telegram, saying, "This just came in from Fort Missoula, Marshal Vail."

Longarm swore softly to himself as Vail tore open the wire. He knew Fort Missoula was the main army post in the Bitterroot country. Vail swore, too, as he scanned the short message from the BIA, sent from a War Department message center. Then he told Longarm, "You'd best be on your way. Last night Weeping Snakes patronized a traveling tent show, or tried to. When they said Indians wasn't allowed to bet agin their wheel of fortune, the Bannock shot the show up and rode off with two captive white gals. The army's given Weeping Snakes twenty-four hours to return the white gals unharmed and pure. The army ain't holding off even that long out of love and charity. They just sent for extra dragoons and guns."

Longarm sighed and got to his feet. Henry held out his travel orders. But Longarm said, "Don't need 'em. Not if I mean to get there in time. The next passenger train north won't be leaving before noon. But there's a long-haul freight I can just about catch if I run like hell!"

# Chapter 3

Longarm made it just in time. It hadn't been easy. From the way folks had stared, one would think they'd never seen a gent running like hell through the downtown streets of Denver. The freight he'd recalled from earlier trips north was just chuffing through the switch yards west of the depot he didn't have time to bother with as Longarm vaulted the fence and cut across the tracks at an angle. It was still nip and tuck near the end. A lesser man might not have made it after running all the way from the federal building. But as the caboose whipped by he caught a grab iron and swung himself aboard the rear platform, panting and cursing considerably.

His mad dash across the yards had of course not gone unobserved from the brakeman's tower atop the caboose. So the rear door opened and a rough-looking gent followed the twin muzzles of his sawed-off twelve-gauge out to inform Longhorn, "All right, bo. You catch trains good. Now let's see how good you jump *off* 'em!"

Longarm wheezed. "Hold your fire, old son. I'm the law. Who's head brake this trip, old Windy Weaver?"

The man with the shotgun shook his head and said, "Windy ain't braking any trains no more. He fell between the cars on the K.C. run a week or more ago, and anyone can *say* they's the law."

Longarm nodded and replied, "That sounds properly cautious for a gent guarding a string of empty boxcars. I'm reaching inside this coat for no more than my buzzer and I.D. now. So would you mind pointing that thing somewheres else?"

"Let's see your I.D. afore we discuss the matter further."

Longarm brought out the official wallet he packed for such occasions and showed the surly brakeman his federal badge and I.D. The brakeman lowered the muzzles of his twelve-gauge with a shrug and said, "All right. We got orders to be polite to tramps of your description. Go on up the catwalk a ways and you're sure to find an empty where you'll be outten our way. Next stop is Cheyenne. If you was planning on getting off anywheres *closer,* tough. We're only stopping at Cheyenne long enough to jerk water."

"I'm trying to get to Fort Missoula in less than twenty-four."

"You hopped the right freight, then. We ought to make Missoula around one or two in the morning. Go on forward and find yourself an empty. The last six cars are sealed, but we're carrying plenty of empty cars back to the mining and cattle country up north."

Longarm nodded but said, "I didn't have time to pick up my saddle, bedroll, and such. When Windy was bossing this combo he let me bed down in the caboose on long runs."

The new head brakeman shrugged and said, "He ain't bossing this train. *I* am! And as long as I am, nobody but train crew gets to use train crew facilities. I'm going back inside now. You do whatever you've a mind to. But it's only fair to warn you we'll be going a lot faster once we clear the city limits."

Suiting surly actions to his unneighborly words, the brakeman turned away to go back inside and slam the door in Longarm's face. Longarm told him what he thought about his mother, too, and made sure everything in his gun rig and pockets was well settled before he moved to the rear ladder and climbed topside.

The view would have been more interesting from atop the train if the catwalk hadn't seemed so intent on moving out from under his army boots as he teetered his way forward. It was jumping across from car-top to car-top that made him most uneasy. But he knew they were watching from the caboose tower behind him. So he made his way forward as casually as the average man might have, with his heart stuck high in his throat. Despite his uneasy balancing act and his annoyance at the crude manners he'd been subjected to, Longarm carefully counted off the cars as he made his way along them. When he got to what was supposed to be the first empty, he kept going to show them he was just as unwilling as they were to be neighborly. But after he'd worked halfway to the engine up ahead, he decided enough was enough. So he moved down the ladder between cars, peered around the outside, and when he saw that sure enough a reefer door was ajar as well as unsealed, he worked his way to it and swung inside.

It was dark in there, after coming in out of the bright morning sun, but Longarm's ears were good, too. So when he heard a startled gasp he crabbed out of line with

31

the half-open door, slapping leather as he lied, "Freeze! I see you, too!"

"Don't hurt me, mister!" a small scared voiced replied. As his eyes adjusted to the dimmer light, Longarm spied a small form huddled in the far corner, knees drawn up to make itself still scarcer. Longarm put his gun away, saying, "It's all right, bo. Lucky for you, I don't work for this rude railroad, either."

The young hobo in the corner gulped. "I don't have no money and I don't go in for sissy stuff. But I'll share half a bottle of Sneaky Pete I got with you, if you promise not to *hurt* me!"

Longarm moved toward that end of the car, scuffing up the thin layer of straw on the planks of the empty as he did so. He kicked a mess of straw into the corner across from the young bo's and took off his coat and hat before sitting down, saying, "I hardly ever beat up kids, kid, and you may need your liquor a lot before this train gets us anywhere important. We'll be in the high country before dark and, no offense, you seem to be traveling light, even for a bo. I didn't think to bring blankets, neither. But, what the hell, it'll get hot as hell in here before it gets cold as ice. My handle is Custis Long and I'm headed for Fort Missoula. It's your turn."

The young bo said, "I'm Jimmy Nolan. I'm trying to get to Fort Missoula, too."

"Do tell? No offense, Jimmy, but you don't look big enough to join the army yet."

"I'm almost eighteen," the young bo blustered.

Longarm was too polite to ask how shy of eighteen they were talking about. He'd joined an army under-age one time, too, although, in truth, the taller teenaged Custis Long who'd told the recruiting sergeant he was twenty-one and didn't need his parents' consent had likely sounded more convincing. He knew it would be a waste of time to try and talk the kid out of it. Lots of older folk had tried to tell him to let the Blue and the Gray fight it out without his fool-kid help, too. He'd wished more than once, before it was over, he'd had more respect for the advice of his elders. But he hadn't, and he'd lived through it and come out a man, so what the hell. Maybe they'd make a drummer boy or kitchen helper out of this poor skinny little runt. He knew they'd *take* him. The army was so desperate for men willing to soldier for thirteen dollars a month that they had recruiters waiting at the docks as the immigrant ships came in.

They rode quite a ways in silence. Then Jimmy asked Longarm how come he was on his way to Fort Missoula. Longarm yawned and said, "Not to join the army. To keep it out of trouble this summer, if I can get there in time. Do you know anything about cows, Jim?"

"A little. I grew up on a farm. Why?"

"They're starting to run cows on the open federal range to the north since buffalo don't roam all that much no more. The price of beef is up this year and most of the Montana spreads are new. So some figure to be short-handed. A cowhand makes about a dollar a day these days. A cavalry trooper draws less'n half that, and gets yelled at a lot even when nobody's *shooting* at him. You look like a bright kid, Jim. Add her up."

Jim Nolan laughed. "I'm not going to Fort Missoula to join the army. I'm looking for my father. He's a civilian scout working out of there. Or at least he *was*, the last time he wrote home."

Longarm took two cheroots from his vest pocket as he asked, "You mean you ain't sure your dad is *there*, Jim? Where's home, and how long ago did he write to anyone there?"

The young bo accepted the cheroot Longarm handed over, but stared at it dubiously before replying, "I was living in Arkansas with my mom till she died six or seven months ago. As to my dad writing regular, he didn't. You see, my folks busted up when I was little, and Mom rewedded. But once and again when I was little my real dad would send a letter and sometimes even money, when it was my birthday or maybe Christmas."

Longarm thumbed a match-head to light both their smokes as he observed, "You sure must want to look your real dad up. What prompted you to this quest by rail? The usual trouble with a stepdaddy once there's nobody about to protect you?"

Jimmy coughed on the cheroot smoke and struggled some to say, "You sound like you've heard my story before, Custis."

Longarm said, "I have, many a time, and sometimes it's even been true. Some step-parents can be pissers. Others just expect a kid they have to support to do some of the chores around the spread, and most of us hates chores even when our *real* parents make us do 'em. How do you know your real dad won't make you bring in the firewood, if and when you catch up with him, and how do you know he's at Fort Missoula in the first place, if he writes so seldom?"

Jimmy tried manfully to inhale on the cheroot, but gagged and almost puked. So Longarm took it back, snuffed it out, and said, "Waste not, want not. Three-for-a-nickel smokes require a little hair on one's chest to inhale on, no offense. He was talking about how you knowed your father would be waiting to meet this train, Jim."

The young bo sighed. "He doesn't know I'm coming. I didn't even leave a note when I ran away. But he did write me about a week ago. He said he'd just heard about Mom's passing and he put a ten-dollar bill in the letter as well. But my infernal stepfather found it in my drawer and said he needed it more'n a sassy kid like me, so—"

"I take back what I said about some stepfathers," Longarm cut in with an understanding nod. "You got the return address off the envelope from your dad, right?"

Jimmy looked blank. "There wasn't any return address. But he said he was on his way to Fort Missoula and that he'd write to me some more when he got there."

Longarm frowned thoughtfully and asked, "You made him an army scout, out of no more than *that,* Jim?"

The young bo nodded and replied, "What *else* would he be doing up that way? He *used* to be an army scout, when him and Mom was wedded. He used to ride off someplace with the army all the time and when I was little I could hear them through the wall, fussing about it. Mom said she was tired of waiting at home alone for him all the time. Then they must have had an awful fight I never heard, because the next thing I knew we moved to another place and Mom said she was married to this *other* son of a bitch!"

Longarm nodded but didn't answer. He'd heard the story all too often for a man who didn't have a happy ending for it. The fool kid would either find his wandering father in Fort Missoula or he wouldn't. Neither outcome could possibly be a federal offense and he hardly ever adopted orphans. So Longarm lowered his head to the arms he'd locked across his knees and tried to doze away the lazy miles between him and more important matters.

It must have worked. For the next thing he knew the train had stopped with a jerk, tossing him over on one side as it woke him up so rudely. He sat up again, rubbed his sleep-gummed face, and growled, "If we ain't been stopped by the James–Younger gang, this has to be Cheyenne."

Jimmy Nolan said, "Be quiet! The brakemen will be checking for hot boxes, and if they hear us in here..."

Longarm chuckled. "I can see you've been talking to lots of older gentlemen of the road since running away, Jim. But I ain't riding sneaky. Let's see if I can get us some provisions, since they seem to have neglected a dining car aboard this train."

As the young bo protested further, Longarm slid the side door all the way open, stared out across the Cheyenne yards, and, sure enough, spied a familiar figure in the distance.

Mammy Jammer, though that could hardly have been her real name, was a motherly colored woman who sold sandwiches and such to coach passengers and train crewmen as often as she could. Her cook-shed and shack were just off railroad property, and the train Longarm had caught wasn't on the regular through tracks. But Mammy recognized his familiar figure at a distance, too, and came over as fast as she could manage, packing her big baskets.

Longarm dropped down to the ballast to greet her. "Howdy, Mammy. I got a couple of dollars to bet that you can't show me enough grub and more important liquids to get two grown men through the tedious miles between here and the Bitterroots."

The heavy black woman's face lit up as she said, "You lose, honey. What you want to drink with these here hams on rye, real beer or soda water?"

Longarm got out his more serious real wallet. "Both," he said. "We'll take all the bottles you got and, let's see, may as well take all your sandwiches, too. It's always

36

best to have more than less. How much money are we talking about, Mammy?"

She hesitated before she said, "Well, I generally charges a nickel a bottle and my sandwiches are a steal at fifteen each."

Longarm told her he didn't have time to haggle. In the end he bought a dozen paper-wrapped sandwiches, six bottles of soda water, and would have bought more than four bottles of beer if she'd *had* more. He had just completed his transaction and placed the refreshments on the doorsill when the same boss brakeman came down the line, wearing a scowl and carrying a wrench, to shout, "Hey, nigger! Get the hell away from my train, you black bitch!"

Mammy Jammer moved off quickly and was almost out of earshot by the time Longarm could object calmly, "She wasn't messing with your train. I called her over. So if you have a beef with anybody it's with *me*. Your move, friend."

# Chapter 4

The somewhat tense discussion had drawn the attention of others, mostly the crew of the same train, so the boss brakeman was aware he had an audience and that he had to play some to it as he growled, "All right, what's done is done. Just don't get wise with me. And, next time, *ask* afore you call anyone over."

Longarm didn't answer. That should have ended it, had the boss brakeman been smarter. But, as he started to turn away, he spied the young bo peeking fearfully out of the interior shadows and, with the sometimes stupid instincts of the born bully, he yelled for all the world to hear, "Son of a bitch! It ain't enough I got freeloading lawmen aboard my train, a fucking *bo* has dared my wrath as well?"

Longarm said, "It's all right. He's with me. Federal witness."

"The hell you say!" the brakeman thundered, and now

men who had no business anywhere near the train were drifting across the yard to see what all the fuss was about. The bully pointed and said, "All right, you little shit, get out here on the double! That's an order!"

Longarm said, "Stay put, Jim. That's an order too."

The brakeman gasped. "Who in the hell do you think you're talking to, mister? In case nobody's told you, they call me Emperor Edwards, and I'm not only the toughest railroader west of the Big Muddy, I'm in command of this here train, too!"

"You tell him, Emperor!" called out one of the younger brakemen.

But Longarm noticed most of the others were just staring bemused as they waited to see what happened next.

What happened next was that Longarm kept his voice low and polite as he said, "This train won't hardly make Fort Missoula any time tonight if we don't get her rolling again. So let's cut this schoolyard stuff and get going again, hear?"

"Not until that bo is left ahint, suitably busted up to learn him a lesson! Get out here, boy. For if I have to come *in* there for you I'll *really* bust you up!"

He started to climb aboard. Longarm placed the heel of a palm firmly against his face and shoved. The Emperor Edwards wound up seated on his ass in the cinders two tracks away. And when he got back up, he still had the wrench in his hand.

Longarm had already removed his hat and coat, so his invitation was obvious to one and all as he calmly unstrapped his gun rig and tossed it aboard with the sandwiches and young Jimmy. The Emperor Edwards moved closer, raising the wrench thoughtfully. But then he noticed that, although Longarm had apparently tossed his .44 aside, twin gun muzzles still seemed to be trained on him. Lots of people had noticed that about Longarm's cold gray eyes when the big deputy was starting to get angry. The smarter ones were still alive, and a man seldom made crew chief by being stupid. So the Emperor Edwards said, "Oh, shit, I ain't allowed to whup federal lawmen, and if you want a punk to keep you company that bad, be my guest. Far be it from me to come betwixt sissy lovers!"

Longarm grimaced, but resisted the impulse to stampede over the foul-mouthed asshole. Longarm was a man who liked to finish fights he started, so he was careful not to start them when he didn't have to. He just boosted himself back aboard and sat there with his feet hanging out of the car door until they started up with another jerk and it was obvious the war was over, for now.

He started to strap his gun rig back around his hips. Then he shrugged and tossed his .44 atop his rolled-up coat in the corner. He tossed a wrapped sandwich to the young bo, but said, "You'd best come get this soda, Jim. The bottles fizz awesome if you toss 'em about in this heat."

The kid did neither. Ignoring the wrapped sandwich Longarm had tossed him, Jimmy Nolan was balled up on one side, crying fit to bust.

Longarm shrugged and turned away to admire the passing scenery as he munched his own ham on rye and sipped more serious beer. The kid had to be fibbing about being almost eighteen. But he had to be more than twelve, and Longarm couldn't recall crying much at *that* age. Of course, he hadn't been a young and sort of delicate-featured boy riding freight trains and trying to keep from being molested by older men at that age, either. It was best to just let the poor little rascal cry it out, most likely.

Kids either learned to take care of themselves or give up such a cheap form of transportation.

It was getting hotter as the train moved across rolling, sun-baked prairie. The smell of Mammy Jammer's sandwiches grew stronger, and Longarm wasn't at all surprised when young Jim crept over to sit in the doorway with him and ask, "How do you open them soda-water caps?"

"Don't you have a bottle-opener blade on your knife, Jim?"

"I don't have a knife at all."

"Jesus, it's small wonder you're worried about protecting yourself. Here, I'll open one for you. Try to make it last. It's all we got to drink for quite a spell."

Jimmy Nolan sure didn't listen good. Longarm watched with one eyebrow raised as the young bo guzzled half the bottle of soda water down at once, dug into a sandwich like a wolf in winter, and polished off the rest of the soda in the time it took Longarm to chew and swallow three times. He shook his head wearily and said, "You sure must have been hungry and thirsty."

Jimmy said, "I was. I haven't had a thing to eat or drink since last night, and that was only an apple I swiped. Could I have another bottle of soda, please?"

"Not yet. You'll only wind up puking it wastefully. Here, I'll give you another sandwich. But after a man's gone longer than usual without water he's got to wet his body back slow and sensible. You ever make chicken mash, Jim?"

"Of course. I told you my stepfather worked hell out of me."

"Ain't talking about chores. Talking about *water*. You pour a whole bucket of water over dry chicken feed and more'n half of it runs off to the ground. You got to dribble the water on slow, letting it soak in no faster than the feed can blotter it up, and in no time at all you got the whole bucket in the mash instead of wasted on the ground. Our innards work the same way. Drink too fast when you're dry and you'll surely piss most of it right on through before it's done you any real good, see?"

"I see. But do we have to talk so dirty all the time?"

Longarm considered before he replied, "I don't recall telling you the tale of the horse thief and the farmer's daughter, Jim. I was only trying to educate you about your plumbing, not to give you no hard-on. I don't know what on earth I'd do with a horny hobo in any case. For unlike some of the dirty old men you've been riding the rails with of late, I only like women."

Jimmy laughed. "I'll bet you've had your way with a lot of them, right?"

"I don't brag about such matters. Eat your infernal sandwich and let's change the subject."

Jimmy did and they did. Longarm found riding with a dumb runaway kid almost as tedious as if he'd been riding alone. But it helped to pass the time away as they swapped the stories of their lives. Longarm's seemed to interest the young hobo a lot, but that seemed only fair. For Longarm found his own life story more interesting by far, even though he already knew most of it. When he said as much, and Jimmy asked him how come he didn't know *all* of it, Longarm said, "No man knows the whole story of his life. For one thing, if a man can still talk about it all, the story ain't *over* yet. But what I really meant was that no man can tell the story, even to himself, as it might be told by others who know him as well or better."

"I don't follow that at all."

"I know. You take your tale of running off from a wicked stepdad in search of your real dad, the wandering hero. I never met any of the others involved. So it's up to you to figure out if your stepdad, your real dad, or even your late mother would tell the story in the same words, Jim."

"How would *you* tell my tale, Custis?"

"I wouldn't even try. Don't know any of you well enough. You'd best study on it some, though. For, when we get to Fort Missoula, if your real dad ain't there, or if he's there and ain't willing to take you in, there's worse things to consider than going home, you know."

"A lot you know," Jimmy insisted. "I'll bet you never woke up in bed with a beery old drunk in bed with you, pawing at your privates and telling you that now that your ma was gone and there was only the two of you left, what was going on was only natural!"

Longarm grimaced, swallowed the beer trying to stay stuck in his throat, and asked, "Jesus, your own stepfather tried to queer you, Jim?"

"He didn't just try."

"You say he was drunk at the time?"

"He was always drunk. Does that give him any excuse to rape me in my ass?"

"Not hardly. It's small wonder you've been acting so goosey, kid. All right, I take back what I said about you returning to the fold. That still leaves us stuck with what happens if your real dad ain't in Fort Missoula when we get there."

"I know. I was hoping I could sort of tag along with *you!*"

"That's all I need. It'd be almost as bad, though a lot more practical, if you was a she-male. When and if I ever decide to raise a family, kid, I mean to start off the

43

old-fashioned way and father my own, no offense. If that won't work, and I *have* to adopt, in the end, I reckon I'd want to start from scratch with someone a mite *smaller,* Jim. But, what the hell, maybe we can get you a job herding cows or something if your dad don't pan out. Meanwhile, I got me some cash to spare. I was only going to spend this getting a brunette drunk enough to kiss tonight anyway. If you can't live on this for a week you're a spendthrift, and if you can't get a job in a week you're just too worthless to worry about."

Jimmy Nolan took the five-dollar bill with a look betraying as much wariness as thanks. But the young bo put the bill away anyhow before asking suspiciously, "What exactly do you expect me to *do* for this, Custis?"

Longarm frowned. "Do? What in thunder could a bitty bo like you do for me? You're supposed to say *thanks,* God damn it! Ain't you got no manners? Do you see any chickens to feed or cordwood to split aboard this infernal boxcar?"

Jimmy repressed a sob. "I'm sorry. Of course I thank you kindly. For you may have just saved my life again. It's just that I ain't used to kindness with no strings attached. You see, the other night a bo I'd rid all day with offered me two bits to, you know, take my britches down and bend over."

"You'd best stop riding the rails, then." Longarm shrugged, putting some of the sandwiches and bottles aside for later. Then he moved to a corner, lay down, and said, "Better try and get some sleep, boy."

Jimmy looked out at the sunny swells of summer-killed short-grass whipping by and protested, "It's too early to think about sleeping."

Longarm said, "You're wrong. We're headed into the high country without a blanket to share or even a newspaper to cover up with between us. It'll be way too cold to sleep in here before the sun's been down enough to matter. So get your rest while you can, kid. By the time this train gets to Fort Missoula we'll be running up and down the length of her to keep from freezing!"

The green young bo was still complaining and sneaking another bottle of soda water as Longarm closed his eyes and willed himself to sleep. It didn't work at first. It wasn't anywhere near his usual bedtime. But he'd fought a war and herded cows in his misspent youth, so he finally managed to drop off and, sure enough, the next time he woke up it was dark outside and getting colder by the minute.

He tried to go back to sleep. Sometimes you could steal a few more winks from the boredom of a night alone. But then he realized he wasn't alone in his corner. Young Jimmy had snuggled up next to him to keep warm, and it was almost working. For, though Longarm's ass against the wall of the car was cold as hell, the young bo felt warmer than most blankets against the front of him.

Longarm started to push the fool kid away. Then he wondered why he wanted to do that. There was nothing wrong with two gents huddled up for warmth with all their duds on, was there?

There was. Longarm couldn't say why. He still felt pure as well as cold and stiff where everything but the young bo was touching him. But the soft warmth of Jimmy's young body felt too nice to be decent. So Longarm knew something wrong was going on inside his head and, not being a man to brood overmuch on such matters, he simply shoved the fool kid away, muttering, "I don't sleep with boys, even sissy boys, damn it."

Jimmy moaned and turned over, still asleep, to snug-

45

gle back against him. Longarm growled, "No, damn it, that's enough." But when he placed a firm hand against Jimmy's chest to shove him away, said chest didn't feel firm at all, though it sure felt *good!*

The young bo awoke with a start to find Longarm's hand on one of her soft young breasts and gasped, "Oh!" You're *touching* me!"

Longarm moved himself and his hand away as much as the wall braced against his spine would let him. "You started it. Why in thunder didn't you tell me in the first place, Jim? And, by the way, what's your real name? You're built too she-male to call Jim, now."

She said, "My real name's Jemima. I thought it best to change it to Jimmy when I bobbed my hair and put on my stepdad's duds to run away in."

"I noticed the cuffs of them baggy britches had been stagged. I can see why you thought it best to pass yourself off a boy while riding the rails, too. But now that your true condition has come to me, you'd best move off a ways, missy."

"It's too cold, and I know I can trust you, Custis."

"You do? Well, you sure must know me better than *I* know me, then! I know you're too young and that we both need a bath and all, but I ain't sure I could stay pure all the way to one or more in the morning cuddled up this way with a real she-male of any description."

She sighed. "All right, why don't we get that part out of the way so's we can lie more relaxed together?"

He blinked in surprise. "Are you always so pragmatical about such matters, sis? You just told me you run away from home because a dirty old man kept raping you, and yet, no offense, if you ain't trying to rape *me*, you're surely acting like you mean to *seduce* me!"

She moved closer as if to prove him right as she said,

"Pooh, I never said I ran away because I hated to be screwed. The mean old drunk kept shoving it in me *backwards* all the time and *that*, damn it, felt hurtsome as well as disgusting."

He laughed despite himself. "Well, you sure don't act like the average virgin. Who broke you in so young, the same wicked stepfather?"

"Of course not. Had he treated me right, I might not have run away. You see, he'd heard a man could go to prison for twenty years for incest in Arkansas. So he was afeared to break my cherry, as he put it. I tried to tell him I didn't mind it frontways. But of course I never dared to tell him I'd been playing doctor with the boys next door, so—"

"Hold on," Longarm cut in. "Did you say *boys,* plural? They sure must breed precocious kids in Arkansas these days. But it may not be too late to save your reputation, if you've only been playing doctor with other children. The only grown man who ever trifled with you never done it to you true, right?"

"I told you my stepfather was afeared to. Of course, there was that hired man we had. But Momma fired him for some reason. I sure wish she hadn't. For it's true a *man* ain't anything like a *boy,* in a hayloft."

"Jesus Christ!"

She ground her pelvis against his in the dark.

"Like I said, it ain't the same with other kids your own age. Say, is what I'm starting to feel agin me through both our pants what I hope it is?"

He sighed and said, "It is. But pay it no heed. It's got a mind of its own. I got a lot more brains in my *head,* though. So I sure wish you wouldn't rub so sassy agin me."

"What's the matter? Don't you *want* to screw me?"

"More than you'll ever know, if the good Lord will only give me the strength. I hope you won't take it personal, Jemima, but your kind suggestion is kind of dumb."

"We're all alone in the dark, and there's plenty of time, honey."

"I know. The twitchy little rascal you're teasing down there keeps telling me the same. But what happens when we get to the end of the line?"

"We get off the train and I look up my real father, of course. Are you afraid I'd tell my own father I wasn't pure?"

"Your mother seems to have figured it out without being told in so many words, Jemima. There's things a gal's parents don't have to be told and, aside from that, you'd be surprised how many gals *do* kiss and tell. I know *I* was, the first time it ever happened to me. Since then I've avoided the problem by just not fooling with gals I could get in trouble over, and an under-aged army brat sure sounds like trouble!"

"Pooh, I told you I was eighteen, almost."

"Almost ain't enough when a gal's daddy has access to a shotgun."

"Oh, for heaven's sake, Custis. I don't want to *marry* you! I just want to keep warm and have some fun."

He wedged his free hand down between them to get out his watch and some matches. There was no way to do so without feeling her fool tits again, and Jemima seemed to take that as a compliment. He ignored her suggestion to explore a mite farther down as he struck a light to see what time it was. He grinned and said, "Hot damn, it's almost midnight! We slept longer than I figured before the cold got through to wake us up. I'm surprised I didn't have wicked dreams, snuggled up with a she-male so long."

"Some of the dreams I was having were wicked enough," she purred, reaching down to fumble with his fly. "We've still got an hour or more, and if we gathered up more hay..."

He sat up, put his watch away, and got to his feet in the dark as she cussed in a most unmaidenly way. It was hard to keep his balance with nothing to fix his eyes on. He put a hand against a splintery wall and moved toward the side door, muttering, "It sure is dark in here. I wonder how come? The almanac says the moon was due to rise full tonight."

Behind him in the dark, Jemima said, "What difference does it make? Can't you enjoy a naked gal's body without having to look at it as well?"

"That ain't our problem right now," Longarm said, running his hand over the door he'd last seen ajar. He couldn't find a handle on the inside. He swore softly. "The son of a bitch has locked us in!"

"Who are you talking about, darling?"

"I ain't your darling, damn it. I'm a U. S. deputy, and the rascal who was afraid to fight one like a man has paid us back with a sneaky trick! I'd have woke if the train had stopped again. He was too afraid of me, even asleep, to enter a dark car occupied by me and my .44. So what the rascal done was to crawl up the train in the dark, slide this door shut, and latch it on the outside."

Jemima crawled over to join him. "Won't somebody open the door when the train stops at Fort Missoula?"

"Not hardly. The only somebody in charge of these empties is the head brakeman who locked us in. Missoula's the end of the line for us. It ain't the end of the line for this freight train. I looked at her dispatches the last time I rode her."

"But surely it has to stop *somewhere*, sooner or later, don't it?"

49

"Yes and no. Once we're in the Bitterroot mining country, north of the fort, they bust up these combinations, dropping off a car here and a car there at mine sidings, cattle-loading stops, and so forth. I reckon the son of a bitch means to run us off the main line at some out-of-the-way cattle station."

"But why, Custis?"

"The fall roundup ain't due until next month."

"Oh, my God! We can't last no month locked up in here without food or water!"

"That's what I just said. This morning I told my boss virtue was seldom its own reward. But this ain't one of them times. For had we wasted time playing slap and tickle in yonder corner, there might not have been time to get us out of this mess."

She asked him what he was talking about. He didn't answer. He was too busy, now that he had his pocketknife out. But when she asked again he realized she couldn't see what he was doing, so he told her. "This door is thick. But it's only wood. If I can whittle a hole big enough to get my hand through in the next hour or so . . ."

"What if he's sealed the latch with that baling wire and lead they use, Custis?"

He kept carving, but sighed and said, "Out of the mouths of babes, or at least out of the mouth of a young bo who's ridden a mess of freight trains recent! I wish you hadn't said that, Jemima. For you may be right, and if you are . . ."

"Don't some of these cars have trap doors in the roof?"

"Only reefers that carry fresh produce. The traps are for ice. This ain't one of 'em. It's just a plain old boxcar meant to carry general merchandise, and there's no way to reach the roof from down here anyway, but . . . hmmm."

He bumped Jemima unintentionally as he moved away

from the locked door. He grabbed her to keep her from falling, and it sure was a wonder how anyone that small could always manage to have a tit between them. "Get back in that corner and stay there," he said. "I'm carrying an open blade in my other hand, and we got enough to worry about in this infernal darkness."

She did as she was told, but naturally kept asking him what he meant to do about the fix they were in. He struck a match. She saw that he was on his knees, peering at the floorboards as he cleared straw away. "I'm looking for nailheads, of course," he said. Then he shook out the match and added, "They ain't hard to find, and there may be other advantages as well."

He folded the cutting blade away and opened the screwdriver blade. Longarm's hands were strong and the old car's floor had seen a lot of abuse. So it only took him a few minutes, and a lot of cussing, to work the first nail out. He felt for the next and swore. "Damn! The head's busted off! But hold on, if the nail ain't got a head it can't be *gripping* important enough to matter. Let's see if the next one over is still willing to be pulled."

"Are you serious?" Jemima gasped as she grasped his intent. "If you pull up the floor, the only way we can get out will be straight down, betwixt the churning wheels, right?"

"Wrong. I hardly ever drop between churning wheels, Jemima. I told you the train stops at Fort Missoula, for a few minutes at least."

It did. Not a moment too late. For even working like a beaver it took Longarm quite a spell to rip up a solid timber floor meant to hold heavy freight. But as the train slowed down a little after one A.M. Longarm peeled the last plank they needed up and tossed it aside. "There we go. Gather your gear together while I find my own. We'll want to drop to the tracks and roll to the dark side the moment she stops. Got that, Jemima?"

"Sure. I've gotten good at dodging yard bulls. But why do *you* have to worry about them? They can't arrest a lawman, can they?"

"They may not know that. I just found out how tedious it can be to argue with morose railroaders. Might have other fish to fry as well. It depends on how things go when the train stops."

Things went surprisingly well as far as Longarm and the girl were concerned. As the train pulled into the Missoula siding and braked to a hissing stop, they simply dropped through the hole in the floor and, noting at the same time that there was a platform flush against the left side of the train, rolled over the track between the wheels and lay side by side in the dirt to see what happened next.

What happened next was that boots came clumping down the loading platform above them and a strange voice called out, "Hey, Edwards, how come you changed the chalkings on this car?"

The more familiar voice of the Emperor Edwards answered, "Keep your voice down. It's late as hell and we don't want to wake nobody up. I'm rerouting this old car to Kate's Crossing because somebody there has some stuff to put in it, of course."

"Do tell? I thought the line had abandoned that siding."

"The *tracks* is still there, ain't they? Don't argue with *me* about it, damn it. I just work for this line, the same as you. Except that, in case you've forgot, I'm the boss of this particular train!"

# Chapter 5

They clumped on, talking about the way the freight was to be broken up. When they were out of earshot Jemima whispered, "You were right! That Emperor Edwards is just plain mean!"

"You just noticed? If I was half as mean I could likely stick him with an attempted murder charge. But I got more important rows to hoe. I got to calm the army and the Indians down before someone really winds up dead. Let's work our way to the shady side of this old platform and find out where the hell we are."

As he helped the now even dirtier little tramp to her feet Longarm looked around to get his bearings. "This ain't so bad. They dropped us off in the *town* of Fort Missoula, not the fort itself. But the military post ain't far and the Western Union ought to be...yeah, *that* way."

As they trudged toward the main street through the

gloom of the trackside shanty town, Jemima asked why he wanted to send a wire at this hour. Longarm said, "Ain't sending a regular wire. It's a heap cheaper to send a night letter my boss can pick up in the more sensible parts of morning. He worries when I don't stay in touch, and I don't want him pestering the railroad about where I might be."

"Oh, wouldn't the railroad pester that mean brakeman about where he let you off if your office wired them?"

"That's what I just said. I'll let Edwards know his joke fell flat when I've time to flatten him proper. Right now I've got a more serious war to stop."

They turned a corner and found themselves on the wider but dusty and unpaved main street of Fort Missoula. He spotted the lamplit Western Union sign a couple of blocks away easily. At this hour only a few lamps burned at all.

They went in and Longarm composed a terse message for Billy Vail. He didn't mention the trouble he'd had with the bully brakeman. Billy always made such a fuss when he hospitalized folk he hadn't been sent out to get. The sleepy-eyed telegraph clerk read the name he'd signed, yawned, and said, "I got a wire for you, too, Deputy Long. It come in around ten-thirty last night. Hold on. I got it here somewheres."

He found it under the counter and handed it across. Jemima looked concerned as Longarm read it, cussing quietly under his breath. She asked if it was bad news.

"Yeah," he said. "They want me to contact an Indian agent here in town named Woodford before I pester either the army or Weeping Snakes, and we're getting mighty close to the deadline for idle conversation."

He balled up Vail's message and tossed it in a handy wastebasket as he added. "Well, at this hour there'd be nobody out to the post awake to talk to but the Officer of the Day, and I learned long ago not to talk to second lieutenants if it could possibly be avoided. If your dad's there scouting for the cavalry at all, they'll have likely sent him and the other scouts out in the field by now. Since Little Bighorn the army's learned to scout an Indian band some before they hit 'em as announced."

He turned to the clerk and asked about the local hotel accommodations. The clerk cast a thoughtful stare at their dusty duds and suggested they try the Drover's Palace. As they approached the barnlike edifice set aside for folk who traveled rough and ready, Jemima asked, "Are we going to check in as man and wife?"

Longarm smiled wryly. "Not hardly. It could ruin *both* our reputations! Let me do the talking and I'll book us adjoining rooms. I'd hire us a bath as well, but I doubt they'll have rooms with such luxuries attached."

He was right. The room clerk hardly glanced up from the book he was reading as Longarm checked them in as two good old boys traveling together and got their keys. The clerk said there was a bathroom down to the end of the hall if they didn't mind sort of tepid water at this hour. Longarm bet him a silver dollar nobody would stoke the boiler at such an early hour and the clerk said he'd lost.

They went on up. Since it was the slow season between roundups, the adjoining corner rooms they'd booked weren't too bad. Jemima, in fact, seemed impressed with the brass bedsteads and clean cotton sheets. She moved to the window as Longarm struck a match to light her lamp. But as she reached for the shade-pull Longarm warned her, "Don't do that, girl. Never look out an upstairs window at night with the light behind you."

She left the shade down. "Who could be gunning for

us at this time of night?" she asked.

He shrugged. "Don't know. But it ain't really night, it's early morn, and since the BIA asked for me in particular by *name* I don't know how many others might be expecting me this morning, either."

"Heavens! Are you expecting Indians to attack you right in the middle of town?"

"Not hardly. But most Indian troubles get started by dumb Indians or smart and sneaky whites, and old Weeping Snakes ain't dumb. I ain't got time to tell you the story of my life again. Just leave that fool shade alone till I find out how welcome we are in this fair city. I got to go out again. Wait a spell, then test the water down the hall, and if the tub ain't iced over total try to scrub yourself down to bare hide. Then lock yourself in here and stay that way until I rap like this on your chamber door."

He rapped out the Morse for CL on the doorjamb twice to make sure she'd remember. She nodded but asked, "Where are you going and how come I can't tag along?"

"They don't serve boys as young-looking as you in most respectable saloons," he said. "I ain't going to get drunk, so I won't be long. I just like to scout some before I turn in in a strange town."

He stared down thoughtfully at her shabby male attire and added, "If nobody's in the hall when you get cleaned up, make a dash back here wrapped in a towel. It'd be a shameful waste of water if you was to put them filthy duds back on. Come morning business hours we'd best get you dressed proper to meet your dad out to the post."

"You mean like a *girl* again?"

"Hell, no, I was figuring to carry you out there dressed as a Cheyenne Dog Soldier. You did say your dad had

56

been writing home to a *daughter,* didn't you? The other scouts would never let him live it down if you showed up in baggy pants."

He consulted his watch, nodded, and said, "All right. I'll see you later, kid. Try to get some sleep in the meanwhile. Come sunup you could have a busy day ahead of you."

He checked his own room out, didn't find bugs in the bedding or anyone lurking in the closet, and went back downstairs. He kept the key in his pocket. The clerk barely looked up as Longarm passed with a silent nod. But the clerk still said, almost talking to the open pages of the book, "Try the Grasshopper around the corner. Don't bring a beer bucket back with you, though. It's agin house rules."

Longarm went on out, strolled to the corner, and sure enough heard a tired rinky-tink piano. The noise was coming from a dimly lit open doorway and someone had hung a big wooden grasshopper above it. So Longarm figured he'd found the right place.

He wasn't so sure when he got inside. The upright piano against the rear wall of the narrow saloon was being tortured by a familiar figure, a mighty nice figure, with long red hair hanging down her back. The barkeep sat half asleep behind a long pine bar stained mahogany. The only two customers were seated at tables against the far wall. One was either asleep or dead drunk. The other one looked like he was having a hard time keeping awake. Longarm had never seen either of their faces on Wanted fliers, so he ignored them as he bellied up to the bar and ordered a schooner of beer with nothing in it. He could see he'd come to the wrong place for local gossip and it was too late, or too early, for serious drinking.

He'd hoped the gal at the piano would just keep play-

57

ing. But she recognized his voice, stopped as if someone had thrown a switch, and got up to join him. As she leaned against the bar with him he nodded and said, "Howdy, Red Robin. I see you beat the charge after all. Or have you escaped some more?"

Red Robin, or whatever her real name was, sighed and said, "I guess I owe you an explanation about that time in Texas, Custis."

He shook his head. "No, you don't. I told you then I only arrest gals who've committed federal crimes, and your piano playing ain't *that* bad. Reckon you just didn't trust me, though, eh?"

The brassy gal sighed again. "I've regretted more than once that I run out on you, just as we was getting to know one another so well. But it's all right now, honey. I got them old charges agin me set aside, so I'm free to associate with the law all I want these days. By the way, my private quarters are just next door, if you'd like to pick up from where we last left off."

Longarm chuckled fondly and said, "Another time, maybe. I got enough to worry about here in Fort Missoula at the moment. But I'd be proud to buy you a drink, Red Robin."

She told the barkeep to give her a double shot of gin and when he mildly pointed out she was supposed to be playing the piano, Red Robin added he could go to hell after he got through serving her. So he served her, muttering under his breath about the boss not liking this at all.

Red Robin clinked her glass against Longarm's beer schooner. "I never get fired for drinking with the customers," she said.

"I thank you for the compliment. I hope you got to drink with more, earlier in the evening."

She took a dainty gulp of straight sloe gin before she nodded and asked, "All right, who are you after this time, Custis? We do get some customers who look like they *ought* to be staring out of reward posters. But I ain't good at guessing games."

"Ain't after white outlaws, as far as I know. They sent me up to have a powwow with the Bannock."

Red Robin grimaced. "I'd best knock off early and take you home for your last good screw, then. The Bannock are on the warpath. So's the army. The main reason it's so quiet in here right now is that all the troopers is confined to the post, waiting for orders to ride out."

"So I've been told. You know many soldiers, Red Robin?"

"Not as well as I know you, if that's what you mean. But, sure, I let lots of 'em buy me drinks. It's my patriotic duty. Why? Are you jealous, I hope?"

He shook his head and replied, "I don't recall buying you a *ring,* that time in Texas. But I'm looking for a gent named Nolan who's said to be working out of Fort Missoula as a scout. Before you say you never heard of him, I'd best add I don't want to arrest him. I got news from home for him."

Red Robin said the name softly a couple of times, shrugged, and screamed, "Hey, Beaver!" loud enough to make Longarm flinch.

It must have startled the half-asleep older cuss at the nearest table, too. For he nearly fell out of his chair as he snapped awake and stared up at them in wonder. He had a full beard and was dressed like a Mountain Man, so the nickname could have fit him either way.

Red Robin said, "Beaver, you're an Indian scout, ain't you?"

Beaver sighed and said, "Well, I ain't no Indian. But

I scouts 'em some for the army. Who wants to know?"

Red Robin introduced him to Longarm, who asked what he was drinking. That brought Beaver to his feet and over to the bar to ha⸲ a bourbon and branch water. He hastily explained to Longarm that he wasn't goldbricking on the job. "Riding out in the dark after Bannock on the prod ain't sensible. Bannock ain't like Lakota. They fights Apache-style, and the cat-eyed sons of bitches can take advantage of a man in the wee small hours."

Longarm nodded understandingly. "All the Ute dialects favor night fighting over daylight cavalry charges. I mean to meet with Weeping Snakes while the sun is shining if I can, too. They still ain't returned the white captives?"

Beaver shook his grizzled head. "Nobody's seen hide nor hair of Weeping Snake's band since they got in that brawl with the tent show the other night. I figure they're holed up in Fool's Gold Valley, if they're still in the Bitterroots at all. I'm *hoping* like hell they've rid over into the Great Basin. I ain't paid to scout *that* fur."

Longarm sipped some beer and said, "I'm looking for another scout called Nolan. Don't know his first name. Forgot to ask. Does he ride on either side of the Bitterroots with you, Beaver?"

The older man frowned thoughtfully. "Can't say as he does. I knowed a *trapper* named Nolan once. The Blackfoot kilt him up near the Canadian line years ago, though. Ain't nobody named Nolan scouting outten Fort Missoula."

"How about some other civilian job, like sutler, blacksmith, hostler?" Longarm asked.

Beaver shook his head again. "Nope. I know all the civilians and officers out to the post by name, and Nolan ain't one of 'em. You sure he ain't one of the kid troopers?

I don't know ever' private soldier by name. We got quite a turnover in the army these days."

"I doubt we could be talking about anyone young enough to be a regular trooper, Beaver. Nolan has a daughter grown to womanhood. Of course, some few unambitious gents has been known to stay in a full thirty years as low-rankers."

Beaver drained the last of his double and stared down wistfully at the empty glass. Longarm pointed at it and as the barkeep replenished the supply Beaver said, "I'd sure like to help you find a man who's worth that much to you, Deputy. But I do know all the old-timers out to the post, being one my ownself, and there just ain't no middle-aged Nolan stationed on or about the military reserve."

Longarm grimaced. "Tell me about Indians, then. Where's this Fool's Gold Valley, and how come it's called that?"

Beaver said, "It's about half a day's ride southwest, depending on what you're riding. Some white prospectors damn near got their fool selves kilt by the Bannock down that way a few years ago. It's the valley Weeping Snakes was born in, and he still includes it as part of his hunting ground, no matter what the Army and the BIA say. But by sheer good fortune the Bannock were off somewheres else when them white boys camped there . . . oh, a couple of years ago. The Bannock would have run over 'em sure had they seen 'em panning in their sacred stream, which is more like a muddy creek when you look at it our way. Anyhow, the prospectors rid back hollering they'd panned color in the crick and traced it to an outcrop further up the valley. But afore a gold rush could get off the ground, the assay office tested the color out as worthless."

61

"Iron pyrites or mica?"

"Hell, how should I know? There's all sorts of glittersome rock a fool can take for gold. I wasn't there. I only heard about it. The BIA had a fit about it, and for once the War Department agreed with the Indian Office. You see, the BIA means to set aside Fool's Gold Valley as part of the Bannock Reserve, if they can ever get the Bannock to hold still long enough to settle anywheres."

"Don't they have an official reservation yet?"

"Sure they do, over in the Great Basin, where they ain't been in recent memory. Weeping Snakes led his band here to Montana Territory after his side lost in the big Shoshone War a year or so ago. He says his medicine is bad in the basin and range country and that the spirits of his mother's clan tolt him they'd look out for him in the greener pastures of the Bitterroots. Mayhaps they do. He surely has been making money hand over fist of late."

Longarm knew the Indian agent Billy had ordered him to contact would know more about the odd situation regarding an official place on the map for the Bannock to be. So he asked Beaver to tell him about the way the Indians were said to be taking advantage of the whites in other ways of late.

Beaver shrugged and said, "I've only seen it happen once. Down in Florence a week or so ago. They helt a fair to raise money for a schoolhouse. One of the booths had this wheel of fortune. You bet two bits a spin and if you won, you got back fifty cents."

"Jesus, the vigilance committee *let* them? Nobody could win at them odds even if the wheel was honest, and I don't think they make wheels of fortune without a brake!"

"Well, it was for sweet charity, and Weeping Snakes beat it all to hell anyways. It was kind of comical. He just stood there wrapped in his red blanket and ever' time they tried to pay him off he just let his money ride and tolt 'em to spin her agin. Two bits don't sound like much, till you start *doubling* it ever' time the same fool number comes up. Weeping Snakes said four was a good medicine number and, for him, it surely was. So he won four bits, a dollar, two dollars, and so forth, till the sweating tinhorns had to beg mercy, pleading that he'd broke the bank. I was the one who explained it to him in his own lingo that even white men didn't have a bottomless supply of gambling money. So he said he'd let 'em keep their hair as he took a good thousand dollars off them and went on down the line to the monte layout."

"How long did it take him to lose his impossible run of luck back?"

"He never. He cleaned out the monte bank, too. Lost the *first* couple of times. Then he throwed back his old gray head and talked to the sky about it some. After that, there was no stopping the rascal. He picked the right card time after time, letting his money ride, till I had to explain again that it wasn't considered civilized to scalp a tinhorn just because he'd run outten money."

Beaver finished his drink, sighed, and added, "I sure wish *I* could talk to spirits like that. Hardly any of the rest of us won enough to matter that day. More than one old white boy was making mighty surly comments by the time Weeping Snakes cleaned out the blackjack gal, too! I got him and his braves to ride out with their winnings afore anyone got kilt, though. Weeping Snakes ain't dumb. Had I been at that tent show the other night, I might have been able to stop that fight, too."

Longarm ordered another round and said, "Before you get ahead to the second incident, let's go back over what you saw with your own eyes in Florence, Beaver. You say Weeping Snakes had some of his braves with him to back his play?"

"Sure, at least a dozen. They'd have likely tolt him he couldn't play had he rid in alone. As it was, there was considerable discussion as to whether Indians was allowed to gamble or not."

"That part's legal, as far as I know. Did any of the other Bannock bet?"

"Nope. Just the old medicine man. Others commented on this. So that's how come I remember. Naturally he had to be cheating. But nobody there could figure out *how!* When he wasn't betting, he kept his hands inside his blanket. None of the other Indians made any sneaksome moves, neither. They all stood back, respectful, as the old rascal skint the white folk shameless!"

Longarm took a thoughtful sip of suds, nodded, and said, "There's no way in hell to beat even an honest house, honest. Now tell me what happened more recent at the tent show. Where was it, for openers?"

"Betwixt here and French Flats, to the north. I only got it secondhand. But, as it was tolt to me by some boys as was there, the old Bannock rid in about sundown, commenced to bet like a maniac, and won like a magician. This time there was nobody to calm his nerves when the gamblers tolt him to take his infernal winnings and git. So somebody pushed a Bannock, the Bannock pushed back, and next thing anyone knew there was considerable noise and confusion. Tables and lamps went flying, a tent caught afire, and more than one shot was exchanged in the tricky light afore old Weeping Snakes called out something and the Indians all headed at once for the pony line. In the confusion some of them rid out on the wrong ponies, which ain't so bad, since they left their own ahint in tacit exchange. But what's got every-

64

body riled is that when order was restored and a head count was taken, two white gals working for the tent show was missing, too!"

"Did anyone really see an Indian ride off with a white gal?"

"Not in so many words. But if the Bannock didn't carry 'em off, who in thunder *did?* They was carnival gals, not soiled doves who might have rid home with some white gent for paid romance. They couldn't have just run off scared on their own, for the locals as well as the tent-show gents searched high and low for 'em all around, and—"

"And the army's given Weeping Snakes until one more sundown to produce 'em alive and well whether they got 'em or not," Longarm cut in. He added, with a morose shake of his head, "I'd best go home and catch a few winks. For I can see I've some riding to do between now and then. I thank you for your words of cheer, Beaver. It's been nice talking to you again, too, Red Robin."

# Chapter 6

Longarm left his modest change on the bar and left. But he'd barely gotten outside when Red Robin joined him, hooking an arm through his as she said, "Let's go get laid afore you chase Indians, honey."

"I thank you for the thought, Red Robin," he said, "but like I said, I got some serious riding to do. I mean aboard a horse."

"Hell, it's only a little after three and you've never lasted more than a couple of hours in my saddle yet."

He chuckled. "Flattery will get you nowhere. But at the risk of flattering you, Red Robin, we both know no man born of mortal woman would be in any shape to rise with the chickens after going to bed with *you* after three in the morning!"

"Will you look me up when you get back, handsome?"

"Maybe, if the Bannock don't cool my passions too much."

"It's a date, then. No Indian born of mortal woman's about to kill you, or treat you half so nice as me, either."

They kissed on it and parted friendly. Back at the hotel Longarm went directly to the bath at the end of the hall, but the water was too cool for comfort. As he forced his shivering behind down under the waves he could still smell the steam from little Jemima's earlier, warmer bath. He told his private parts to simmer down as he washed himself reasonably clean, rinsed off, and dried with a rough towel that didn't look like it had been used too recently. There was no sense getting dressed again, now. He wrapped the damp towel around his middle and carried his things down the hall with him. Then he saw the light coming from under the door of the room he'd hired.

He fumbled under his clothes of his gun rig and got out the .44. He already had the key in his free hand. He moved silently to the door on his bare feet and eased the key in the hole. He tried not to make any noise as he turned it. Then he saw that the damn fool door hadn't been locked in the first place, and he had to turn the key the other way. When he'd done so, he moved in fast, dropping everything but the .44 as he trained it on the figure staring wide-eyed at him from the bed across the room. He lowered the muzzle and kicked the door shut behind him, muttering, "That's a good way to get shot, Jemima."

The little hobo didn't look anything like a boy now. Her face was a lot prettier, washed clean and not peering out from under a battered man's hat. The rest of her looked even more girlish. For she'd climbed into bed naked as a jay and the top sheet was down about her hips as she gasped, "Oh, it's you! For a moment you gave me a start!"

He growled, "I was sort of startled to see you here,

too. I booked you the room next door. How come you ain't in it?"

"Don't you think that's a mighty silly question, darling?"

He laughed despite himself, picked up his scattered things, and tossed them on a dresser before he put the .44 on the bed table next to the lamp, sat down, and trimmed the too-bright illumination. She'd had the lamp burning as bright as it could go and so even with the flame out the mantle of fireproof screening glowed faintly, and as he turned to join her under the top sheet her fresh-scrubbed skin glowed an inviting shade of ruby. He sighed and said, "Well, Lord, you know how hard I've tried. But a man can only stand so much."

As he took her in his arms, the sassy little farm gal giggled and reached down between them to fondle him back. Then she gasped and said, "Oh, dear! Perhaps I spoke in haste!"

"Oh, *hell!* I ain't up to the shy virgin speech right now, Jim."

"I never said I was no virgin. But I fear my experience has been limited to men built more normal and, wait, hold it, we ain't never gonna get that in me!"

But he could feel she was mighty wet where it counted for such a shy little thing. Thanks to her earlier temptations, Red Robin's open proposition, and the way he'd missed out entirely with the barmaid at the Parthenon as well, Longarm was in no mood to argue. He just rolled the little sass on her back, wedged her now trembling thighs apart with his own, and got right down to basics.

As she felt him entering her, Jemima pleaded, "Take it easy!"

As he settled down atop her, Longarm saw she was smaller all over than most gals, so he kept most of his weight on his elbows to be polite as he asked if he was too heavy for her. She didn't answer. She was rolling her head wildly on the pillow from side to side as she bucked her trim pelvis up to meet his every thrust. So he moved his hands down to cup a firm young buttock in either one as he pulled her up to him and let himself go.

When they came up for air, Jemima asked him what was so infernally funny. He kissed her and stayed in her as he said, "I was just thinking how the Lord rewarded me for not yielding to temptation earlier."

She hugged him down against her closer and wrapped both legs up around his waist as she giggled and replied, "I'm glad we saved this for a real bed with all our duds off, too. This would have likely kilt me, with my spine against bare planking. But this feels grand. Could we do it some *more,* dear?"

They could and they did, in some positions Jemima said she'd never even heard of before, although by now it was obvious she'd had a lot more practice in such matters than even she let on. After she'd come on top and collapsed weakly down against him, Longarm decided she was old enough to be told the facts of life. So he told her of his talk with Beaver. Jemima sure carried on when she found out her father didn't seem to be stationed at Fort Missoula after all.

"Oh, Custis, what am I ever to do? I have to find my dad! I can't go back to that mean old drunk."

"Easy, easy, now, honey." He held her closer as he added, "Going back to that old fool would be a pure crime against nature. I've been thinking about your future. You ain't been fibbing to me about your age, have you? I don't like to be suspicious, but I just met another gal in town who not only lied but pulled a gun on me one time."

69

"You've got another girl here in Fort Missoula? I'll scratch her eyes out! I'll snatch her bald-headed! God damn it, I seen you first!"

"That's the spirit. Spoken like a true woman of the West. Forget about other gals. You're the only one I'm in bed with at the moment. The reason I need to know your true age is that there's two ways to work it. I know Miss Morgana Floyd, the headmistress of a decent orphanage down Denver way, and—"

"How *well* do you know this other woman?" she cut in.

Since Longarm thought it wrong to kiss and tell he assured her, "Not *this* well. But she hardly ever beats her orphans. I recall another runaway I left with old Morgana one time. And before you ask, no, I never; the kid was a lot younger than you. Are you really more than sixteen?"

"I told you I'd soon be eighteen. Can't you tell?"

"Not hardly. Gals mature a mite ahead of us poor rascals. You could surely convince most men you're full-grown. I don't think the Arvada Orphanage would take in a gal going on eighteen, damn it. But there's another way to skin the cat. I can give you a note to an agency that gets jobs for gals in Denver. Do you have any skills? Aside from this one, I mean. I ain't about to send a gal so young to Emma Gould!"

She said she was willing to do anything at all to keep from being sent home to her wicked stepfather. As if to show her sincerity, she proceeded to kiss her way down his belly, dismounting in the process, to kiss him in a manner even the gals at Emma Gould's charged extra for.

Longarm started to tell her he didn't want a French lesson. But the harder she sucked the dumber that sounded, so he just lay back and enjoyed it until she'd re-inspired him for more old-fashioned loving.

Longarm wasn't sure he was ready to get rid of her, for such willing bed partners were as rare as hen's teeth, if a man insisted on them being good-looking as well. But he knew he had to send her back to Denver long before they could possibly get tired of each other.

He let himself go and when she said she was coming, he believed her and returned the compliment in kind as her tight muscles clamped almost painfully tight on his ejaculating shaft.

He rolled back beside her and thumbed a match-head for a smoke. As the match flared, Jemima pleaded, "Oh, don't light the lamp! I can't face you now!"

He said, "Ain't lighting no lamp. Lighting a cheroot. It didn't feel all that awful to me, honey."

But she sobbed on, "I don't know what came over me!"

He pulled her closer, nestling her head against his shoulder as he smoked with the other hand. "Working as a lawman, I get to hear stories Queen Victoria and her admirers might not," he told her. "You know why it's so hard to get some women to press rape charges, Jemima?"

"Because they're ashamed to allow they've been fucked?"

"Well, that too, of course, and most gals really do hate it when a gent they ain't been properly introduced to screws 'em painful. But more than one rape victim's confided in me, after some pressing on my part to swear out the fool warrant, that she ain't sure she'd feel right about it, since she feels sort of guilty and mixed up in her head."

Jemima snuggled closer. "Well, I wish I had such a good excuse. But I can't hardly say my stepfather raped me, right out."

Longarm said, "Sure he did. The charge is *statutory*

71

rape in his case. Kids and Indians don't have to be raped by *force* for the charge to stick. They got less say in the matter, see?"

"Oh, good. Then you could come back to Arkansas with me and arrest the brute, right?"

"Not hardly. Unless you have Indian blood, he never committed no federal offense. I ain't paid to enforce Arkansas law, which may be just as well, since *I* may have just raped you statutory there as well. Lucky for us, though, sixteen is the age of consent in the federal territories, and it ain't like I trifled with you so early in life."

She reached down to fondle him. "I don't feel so guilty now, for some reason. Could we do it some more, dear?"

He chuckled. "We'd best sleep on it. Got a long day ahead, and it'll be dawn all too soon, as it is."

"I don't feel at all sleepy, Custis, and we did get some sleep on the train, remember?"

He started to tell her he was tired even if she wasn't. But then, as she kept jerking him off, he wondered why anyone would want to tell a pretty little gal such an awful fib. So he just put out his smoke and got back aboard until it was starting to get light out again.

# Chapter 7

Since Jemima was as contrary as the rest of womankind, if not more so, she was naturally sound asleep and struggling to stay that way by the time the shops had opened downstairs. Longarm had hired their rooms until noon, in any case, so he left the pretty little thing to snore as he took care of some errands.

He bought her a one-way ticket to Denver at the depot but he didn't waste time at the nearby Western Union, since he had nothing more to tell the home office. They already knew he'd made it to Fort Missoula by now, despite the Emperor Edwards, and it seemed doubtful anyone else up this way could be gunning for him yet.

He found a she-male notions shop open and went in to buy Jemima some more suitable traveling duds. The old lady in charge said she was sure the summer frock and sunbonnet would fit better if he brought his young lady in. She sort of blushed when Longarm said he knew the young lady's dimensions as well as anyone. But she took his money and wrapped everything up in brown paper without further argument.

He took the package back to the hotel and let himself in with the key. Jemima was lying on her back and she'd kicked off the top sheet, but she was snoring loud as hell, so he resisted temptation. He tore a couple of sheets out of his notebook and wrote two notes, one to the employment agency in Denver and another to Jemima, telling her what to do when and if she ever woke up. Then he locked the door from the inside, placed the key atop the note and bundle for Jemima, and jumped out the window. The only person outside who seemed to notice was a cowhand taking a piss against the wall as Longarm landed near him, got back up, dusting off the knee that had touched dirt in landing, and said, "Howdy. They was mopping the stairs."

The cowhand just cussed as Longarm turned and strode off. There was a lot to be said for traveling light, but it was time to study on getting himself a saddle and something to put under it. He'd left his bedroll and Winchester behind in Denver, too.

First things being first, Longarm went back to the main street, found the livery stable, and bet them nobody wanted to carry him out to the army post by buckboard. He lost. It only took a little while to get out there. He paid off his bet at the gate and strode on in after flashing his badge at the sentry on duty there.

He reported first to the orderly room to be polite and to see what the army was up to today. The CO was still asleep, or at least not ready to get up yet, being a happily married man with quarters across the parade. The young shavetail acting as Officer of the Day said he'd be proud to lend the Justice Department a cavalry mount and saddle

74

if Longarm would sign for it. So he did, asking at the same time how soon they figured to ride out themselves after Weeping Snakes.

The OD said, "This evening, if our scouts can tell us where he is and he hasn't returned his captives unharmed and pure." He smiled crookedly and added, "As pure as carnival gals come, of course. The old man says having the regimental surgeon examine them for virginity would probably be a waste of time."

"Your CO sounds like a sensible gent. I talked to one of your scouts last night. He told me Weeping Snakes holes up at times in a place called Fool's Gold Valley. How do I get there from here?"

The OD shook his head. "He's not there. A Crow who scouts for us as well already looked. I can't say I'm surprised. Would *you* kidnap two gals and carry them home to the address the Indian Agency has on file?"

"Not hardly. But if the Bannock ain't on their official stomping grounds, where do you reckon they are, Lieutenant?"

"I told you. We don't know. Nobody's seen Bannock one since the brawl the other night, and that was north of here, not south towards Fool's Gold Valley. The Indian agent might know of other campgrounds Weeping Snakes favors. Miss Woodford gets along suprisingly well with the old medicine man, considering."

Longarm frowned. "Did you just say *Miss* Woodford, as in *she-male* working for the BIA?"

The OD nodded and said, "I did. I thought it was sort of funny when I first met her, too. But Miss Woodford seems to know what she's doing. Don't know how on earth she got the job. But she does speak Bannock and they seem to respect her, despite her skirts. Her office is back in town, near the depot. The government hasn't settled on a regular Bannock Agency yet. Not even Miss Woodford can get the moody redskins to settle down in one place. The old man says he thinks it's because the Bannock got horses later than some tribes and may not have learned to say Whoa yet."

"I just said your CO sounds like a sensible gent. The Bannock was wandering rascals back when they was still Digger Indians like their Paiute cousins. They got ponies off their other cousins, the Shoshone, just in time to complicate the California Gold Rush some. But the free roaming days of the Horse Indian are coming to a close, whether we like it or not."

"We?" asked the shavetail with an upraised eyebrow. "The War Department can't get the rascals dismounted and living reserved soon enough. Policing Indians on foot is a lot less work."

Longarm shrugged. "Don't bank on it this summer. The Shoshone and their allies up this way don't know they're licked yet and the Nadene bands we call Apache may have some fight left in 'em before this century winds down. But we ain't going to settle the matter jawing about it in this here orderly room. So I'd best pick out a horse and look this lady Indian agent up."

They shook on it and the OD told him to see Sergeant Hoskins over to the corrals about it. The day was still young as Longarm crossed the dusty parade, but it was shaping up to be a scorcher, for the high country. He took off his coat and draped it over his left arm. When he got to the stables he poked about in the shade of the overhang until he found the burly Sergeant Hoskins in the tack room, seated on a keg in one corner, with a pink *Police Gazette* in one hand and a bottle in a brown paper bag in the other. When Longarm told him who he was and why he'd come, the boss hostler bellowed till a young private came in with a stable fork in one hand. Then the noncom said, "Compten, get this gent a horse and saddle. I'd do it myself, but my back's bothering me again this morning."

The private didn't argue. Nobody had expected him to. Longarm picked up the cavalry saddle and bridle he would need right there in the tack room and followed Compten outside to see what kind of horseflesh they were riding in these parts.

Longarm draped the saddle over a corral pole and lashed his tweed coat to it behind the cantle as he eyed the cavalry mounts milling aimlessly on the far side. He said, "That bay with the white blaze looks tolerable, Trooper." "It ought to," Compten said. "It's the colonel's private mount. You'd best pick another."

"I ain't got time for guessing games, old son. Suppose you pick me one as ain't spoken for by anyone important."

The soldier said, "That bobtailed roan mare ain't been issued to anyone yet."

"Don't issue her to anyone you don't want to lose on the trail, then," Longarm said. "Can't you see her withers is weak? What about that buckskin with white stockings, yonder? He looks like he's got some Indian blood. A thoroughbred-mustang cross rides tough as well as sudden."

"Oh, you don't want Rainbow. He's only half broke. The remount service did buy him off a spread in Wyoming, as a matter of fact, and despite his nice lines, they got took. Old Rainbow just ain't cut out to be a soldier."

"Do tell? How come you call him Rainbow? He ain't colored all that unusual."

"He gets his name from his habit of trying to go *over* the rainbow unexpectedly. This can be sort of discon-

77

certing when the outfit's on dress parade. So the colonel says he needs more breaking, or a bullet in his head if that don't work."

Longarm nodded and said, "In that case nobody ought to get too riled if I lose the critter in my travels. You got a throw rope handy? Somehow I don't reckon he's the kind of pony who comes over to get petted when you whistle to him."

Longarm was right. Compten produced a coil of grass rope from a nearby corral post and Longarm climbed into the corral before he took it with a nod of thanks. All the mounts had, of course, seen a man with a rope in his hands before, so they commenced milling about and stirring up considerable dust as Longarm shook out a loop and tried to sort the buckskin out of the confusion. He noticed Rainbow was smart enough to keep other, dumber mounts between him and that throw rope as they all churned about on the far side of the corral. Longarm admired smart horses. But *he* was smart, too. He got the loop whirling, staring away from Rainbow as if he meant to rope the CO's bay. Then, aiming with the corner of his eye, he sent the loop over the back of another bay to settle around Rainbow's thick neck.

Rainbow didn't like it much. He fought like a four-legged trout as Longarm reeled himself, rather than the much heavier gelding, in to meet near the center of the corral. As they got close enough to one another to matter, Rainbow decided that since fighting the rope didn't seem to be working, he'd try fighting the man who'd roped him.

He made his move too late. Longarm was too close and too big in his own right for the buckskin to rear up and box with his steel-shod hooves. But since he wouldn't stop trying, Longarm had to show him the error of his

78

ways by whipping him across the eyes a few times with his Stetson.

Rainbow gave up, or pretended to, and allowed Longarm to lead him to the rails and even put the saddle and bridle on him. As Compten cinched the saddle for him while he steadied the brute's barrel head, he noticed some other soldiers were drifting over to watch the fun.

One of them called out to Compten, "Who's the fool you've stuck with old Rainbow this morning?"

"He ain't a fool," Compten called back. "He's a deputy marshal in need of transportation."

"He's still a fool, then. Rainbow ain't transportation. Rainbow is more what one could call a complexicated and needlessly uncomfortsome form of suicide!"

The friendly young trooper told Longarm, "He's got a point, you know. It ain't too late to choose another mount, Deputy."

Longarm said, "Sure it is. It took long enough to saddle and bridle this one! Open the gate for me, will you? I want to mount up away from his cheering section, and he's fighting the bit already, cuss his sweet hide!"

By the time they'd managed to get Rainbow out of the parade the audience had grown. Longarm even saw some ladies standing on the veranda across the way with some officers. He patted Rainbow soothingly. "Well, Rainbow, I know you have a rep to keep up," he said, "but I don't like to get bucked on my ass in front of she-males, neither. So we shall see what we shall see."

He mounted so swiftly and so gracefully for such a big man that he was well settled in the saddle before the rogue gelding could get set to register a complaint. But then Rainbow made up for lost time by heading straight up and, had not the Montana sky been clear and cobalt blue all around, he'd have likely at least come close to any rainbows up there.

"Kee-rist!" bellowed a distant authoritative voice as Longarm and Rainbow gyrated around and mostly high above the parade, "who issued that killer to a poor be-nighted civilian?"

Longarm was too busy at the moment to inform the colonel it had been his idea. As the rogue bucked every damned direction but civilized under him he was wondering, himself, why he'd ever had such a fool notion. He'd come out here to get a horse to ride, not to put on a Wild West show for free. But as long as gals were looking, and Rainbow wanted to show-boat for them, he figured he might as well show-boat for them, too. He wasn't as big and mean as Rainbow, but he was older, and he'd been around this bush more often. So he kept whipping the brute with his hat as they went up and down in a cloud of dust, shouting, "Come on, Rainbow, you can do better than that! Do you just mean to crowhop like a sissy, or do you mean to really *buck?*"

Rainbow tried. His worst trick was leaping high in the sky to come down like a duck hound trying to shake himself dry coming out of the water. The first time Rainbow did it Longarm thought he was going off for, sure, and he would have if his legs hadn't been longer than average. But Longarm's legs were strong as well as long and once he had a scissors grip on a critter it was a bitch to pry him loose. This was slowly sinking in as Rainbow tried his best and failed to dislodge a rider who was sort of heavy to carry through the sky as well. So the bronc gave up for now with a defiant stamp of a foreleg and an angry shake of his head even as Longarm popped the bit back in place behind Rainbow's molars, where it belonged, with a sudden sneaky jerk. He took advantage of the minimal control he now had to crank the big gelding's head around to the left as he waved his hat at the crowd and said, "We're going out that gate, now, Rainbow. Unless you want me to kick the shit out of you."

The buckskin tried to save at least some pride by tear-assing at the gate at a dead run. Since Longarm was headed that way in any case, he let him. They tore down the road to town a quarter of a mile or so and then Rainbow, as if he missed his audience, tried to slow to a more comfortable lope. But Longarm heeled him hard, whipped his rump with the rein ends, and said, "Not hardly. You *started* this, you fool speed demon. So we'll just keep running till *I* say it's time to slow down, hear?"

He ran Rainbow all the way back to town and, had horses been able to cry and plead for mercy, Rainbow likely would have long before Longarm slid him to a dusty stop in front of the livery, dismounted, and called to the stable boy in the doorway, "I want this mule-headed bastard rubbed down and oated. Easy on the water, though. I'll be back directly and he'd better not be bloated."

The youth took the reins. Rainbow was too grateful to argue. The young hostler patted his muzzle and told Longarm, "You sure are rough on horses, mister."

Longarm nodded, but said, "That's fair. This horse is rough on mankind, too. Watch out for sudden changes in his disposition as soon as he's got his wind back. We can settle on how much I owe you when I come back to find out how much damage he's done your stalls."

He went next to the railroad depot to ask directions. They steered him to the same mustard-yellow frame building the Western Union was in. The temporary Indian agency was upstairs. That made it handy. He didn't bother to see if anyone had wired him recently. He was already on the scene and he still didn't know much more than he had leaving Denver.

As he approached the building a moon-faced individual dark enough to pass for a full-blood but dressed white came around a corner at him, looking sort of guilty about something. Longarm hadn't seen his face on any Wanted fliers, though, so he just nodded politely. The Indian looked right through him and kept going. Longarm shrugged and turned the same corner to see that, sure enough, an outside stairway led to the top floor around the side of the Western Union.

But before we could go up, a gal was coming down. She looked like she was in a hurry. She looked sort of handsome, too, if a man was tall enough for gals as beanpole-tall as she was. She looked too tough to describe as willowy. Her brown hair was bunned severely under a black Spanish sombrero. Her mannish white cotton blouse looked cool for riding, if a mite open at the neck for a proper Victorian miss. She had on a split riding skirt of black whipcord that would have been scandalously short had not her exposed ankles and shins been encased in tooled Mexican boots with jingle-jangle silver spurs to go with them. He could tell from the way she'd lashed the spurs with rawhide latigo thongs that her spurs were meant more for serious riding than for show. He ticked the brim of his pancaked Stetson to her and said, "I'm looking for Miss Woodford, the Bannock agent, ma'am. Is that her office up there where you just come from?"

"It is, and I'm her. Are you Longarm? You fit the description they wired me," she replied.

He pleaded guilty and asked what other awful things they'd said about him. She almost smiled as she replied, "You're said to treat Indians fair-minded. We may be on the same side, after all. White men who even *try* to understand Indians are pretty rare."

"As rare as white *women* who understand 'em, ma'am?"

"I knew you were going to ask that. All right, I was born and reared in the Great Basin and I had more Digger Indians than dolls to play with, growing up. So I speak most of the Ho dialects pretty good and the BIA finds it hard to find whites of either sex who can. Most whites who savvy any Indian at all only know the more familiar Algonquin dialects. The Bannock don't speak Algonquin and they told the last agent so, loudly, when he tried addressing them in what he thought was their own lingo."

Longarm nodded understandingly. "Nearest Algonquin speakers would be the Siksika and, in the Shining Times, Siksika and anyone talking Ho took aim at one another on sight."

This time she did smile as she marveled, "Good Lord, you didn't call them *Blackfoot* and you know what *Ho* are, too?"

"Yes'm. Ho means 'person' or just plain folk to the nations as speak it. They calls us Saltu and we call them Bannock, Shoshone, Ute, or Paiute, depending on who described 'em first. Hopi, Comanche, and them old Aztec down Mexico way all talk Ho, too. I must say some branches of the family have different customs . . . no offense."

"Are you saying the Bannock are wild Indians?"

"Unreconstructed would be a more delicate way to put it, don't you reckon? You know 'em better than me. But I have heard tell Bannock ain't quite as peace-loving as their Hopi cousins, or as harmless as the Digger tribes farther west, come to study on it."

"Weeping Snakes doesn't want another war. I'd stake my life on it, Longarm."

He shrugged and said, "You may be doing just that, ma'am, if you're headed right now where I suspicion you're headed."

She frowned thoughtfully up at him and asked, "Who

says I'm going anywhere right now, Deputy?"

"The riding outfit you got on, and the Indian who just rode in dressed white to tell you where Weeping Snakes and the others was holed up, of course."

She sighed. "You *are* as good as they say you are. But I'd still better meet with them alone. They trust me. They don't know you, and you did fight on the other side in the Shoshone War, you know."

"Sure I know. I was there. Weeping Snakes and me has met in battle, and so we ought to respect one another. I know *I* respect *him*. If he don't respect me, that's *his* row to hoe. I ain't letting no she-male citizen of these United States ride alone into a camp of Indians classified at the moment as Hostiles. So you can ride in with me side by side, or you can ride in with me trailing and covering you. It's up to you, ma'am."

She shook her head. "Damn it, I told their herald I was coming alone, not with an armed escort Weeping Snakes remembers as an army scout!"

"Heck, I ain't all that armed, ma'am. I ain't got my saddle gun with me. As to my being an ex-scout, that's fair. Weeping Snakes used to be a war chief and, while I can prove I ain't riding for the army these days, he's still got two white captives to explain if he insists he ain't at war with nobody."

Miss Woodford stamped her not-so-tiny foot to ring her spur and insisted, "It's all a misunderstanding. The Bannock aren't holding those two missing fancy gals. I know that for a fact!"

"No, you don't, ma'am. You've taken the word of Weeping Snakes he ain't got 'em. Neither one of us has looked under all the blankets at his camp for 'em. Where do you keep your mount, and how far do we have to ride?"

She said, "My pony's at the livery, of course. But you can't come."

He laughed. "Sure, I can. My mount's there, too. So why don't we cut out this fool fussing and get to it?"

"Oh, you're just impossible!"

He agreed, pointing out how impossible it was for her to ride off anywhere without him. So in the end they rode out together, with her still telling him he couldn't come with her. She didn't get it, or at least she didn't let on she did, when Longarm said they could talk about him coming with her after they'd talked to the Indians.

# Chapter 8

The Bannock or Horse-Paiute had been named by Mormons exploring the headwaters of the Snake River a spell back. One could swallow the Book of Mormon whole or take it with a grain of salt, but Joseph Smith's revelation that the American Indians were a lost Tribe of Israel, and hence human beings, had certainly simplified the way the Latter-Day Saints got along with Indians. The so-called Bannock the Mormons had managed to make contact without losing too much hair had hitherto been classified by the less understanding Mountain Men along with the other Ho-speaking tribes in the area as just plain Snake Indians.

Bannock was as close as the early Mormon scouts could get to "Pan-Iti" as the Indians themselves identified themselves. According to Miss Woodford, who knew them even better than the Mormons by now, it was even more correct to call them Pan-Iti-Nehmeh or Paiutes of

86

the North. Longarm said he'd try to remember that, but he didn't really mean to stew his brains about it. The Bannock were already sort of confusing as well as likely confused Indians.

For anyone could see that the good Lord had intended all the Paiute clans to wander the Great Basin as nomadic food-gatherers or Digger Indians, hunting here, digging for roots there, picking pine nuts somewhere else, and never camping more than a week or so in one place. But the Wind River Shoshone had borrowed the High Plains Horse Culture after wandering over the Great Divide by accident one time, and so first the other Shoshone and then their Bannock cousins had started acting like half-ass Lakota or Absaroke to confuse both sides. Like the so-called Apache to the south, Shoshone and Bannock fought like dragoons or mounted infantry, at night, instead of by day like Plains Indians, which was one reason upset whites tended to call them sneaks or snakes. The Indians themselves called *other* bands they didn't approve of sneaks or snakes. So the man they were going to see had gotten his name as a youth by hitting so many Salish on the head after a misunderstanding about horses that the Bannock at least bragged the Salish or Snakes had been left weeping.

But at the moment Weeping Snakes was camped on the wrong side of the Bitterroot divide to pester Salish, although he seemed to be fretting hell out of the white folk in Montana. Miss Woodford led Longarm to a whitewater mountain creek crossing the trail and then up along it, saying, "They've made camp above the ghost town, about the springs feeding this creek. You'd best not come any farther."

He ignored her suggestion but asked what ghost town they were talking about.

"It was called Kate's Crossing, I think," she said. "The mine bottomed out long before I got here. During the gold rush of the Sixties, fools sank mines anywhere they could swing a pick. But the Bitterroots don't have the same foundation rocks as the real mining country in the Anacondas running cross-grained to them. So, after the first wild rush, the Bitterroots were given back to the cowboys and Indians, with a lot of treacherous try-holes dug in their slopes, of course."

Longarm was only half listening. He knew the history of Montana Territory already. But it was interesting that the Emperor Edwards had routed the boxcar he and Jemima were supposed to be locked up in to a total ghost town. That made it premeditated murder, when, not *if*, he ever met up with the son of a bitch again.

The creek purled under a rail trestle ahead and as they came to it, sure enough, Longarm spied a familiar barn-red boxcar on a spur siding near some even more beat-up shacks and a loading platform someone had half salvaged for lumber. Miss Woodford said, as they rode up the bank and into the ghost town, that there was nothing of interest left in any of the deserted buildings. He told her to rein in and he drew his .44 anyway, saying, "I'd best scout ahead some, ma'am. Don't worry about me gunning any of your pet Indians. I've reason to consider ornery *whites* hereabouts. There's a limit to how long even a boss brakeman can leave railroad property out here in the middle of nowhere."

She glanced back at the boxcar they'd just passed. "I don't see anything unusual about that old railroad car. You can see it's empty from here," she remarked.

He nodded grimly and replied, "I know. Someone opened the side door wide, and likely got an uneasy surprise. I'll just drift on ahead and . . . Never mind, that pony dropping next to the steel-shod hoofmarks in the dirt ahead says he rode in alone and, yep, rode out the same way, sudden."

"Who on earth are you talking about, Longarm?"

"Just a skunk you've never met, ma'am," he replied, not wanting to tell her the full story, since it would take a lot of time. By now Jemima would be on her way south to Denver, so he didn't have to worry about her meeting a mean freight brakeman on the passenger combine and, hell, the bully would never recognize the young hobo he'd tried to kill in a sunbonnet anyway. Longarm tried to picture little Jemima in that print summer frock he'd bought her, but it wasn't easy.

They rode on. The stream cut through a rock cleft they had to ride well around. On the far side, in a parklike glade, a circle of half-ass tipis covered with white cotton duck instead of buffalo hide was set up around the big pond the creek poured out of to the east. No Indians were in sight, so Longarm knew they'd been spotted coming this far. Beyond the tipi ring a fair-sized remuda of ponies was confined to a rope corral. From out of the tipi ring came a pack of small yaller dogs pretending to be wolves after elk. He could see Miss Woodford had visited Indian camps before when she ignored them too. Indians ate dogs that bit. But old Rainbow, despite his Indian-pony blood, decided about then that the safest place to be was somewhere up in the sky where the pesky dogs couldn't follow.

Indians enjoyed a good show as much as anyone. So by the time Rainbow and his cussing rider were halfway through their renewed contest the whole band, man, woman, and child, was gathered about in a wide circle, laughing fit to bust as Longarm whupped the lathered buckskin with his hat and called him awful names. He savvied just enough Ho to suspect that more than half the crowd was rooting for old Rainbow to buck him on his head and stomp it flat. But by now he had most of Rainbow's tricks down pat and he managed to disappoint them. The buckskin stopped bucking as soon as he figured out there had to be a better way to kill such an experienced bronc rider. Longarm hit him a couple more licks and then dismounted to hold the reins close with his left and punch the fool horse in the muzzle with his right.

Behind him Miss Woodford said, "Oh, that's cruel!"

He turned to see her standing dismounted next to an Indian pretending to be a snow-covered pine wrapped in a new red blanket.

Longarm nodded and said, "Howdy, Weeping Snakes. I don't know if you remember me, but we met down by the South Pass one time."

The white-haired, six-foot-seven Bannock nodded politely. "I remember you, Longarm. *You* missed *me,* too! Why don't you shoot that horse? Anyone can see he has a bad heart."

Longarm said, "He may be a mite frisky, but I hate walking even more. I'll join you and your agent directly, Chief. I'd best tie this ornery critter to a stout tree, away from your own ponies."

As he led Rainbow away, he heard Weeping Snakes behind him growling, "Hear me, I am no longer a Moho. I am a Tlamatinimay, now."

Longarm didn't want to argue about it. He led Rainbow off to a stout enough looking lodgepole pine with some Bannock kids tagging along, chattering at them admiringly. It wasn't clear whether they were telling him he was a fair rider or telling Rainbow what a great pony he was. But, like most warrior societies, Bannock had little use for a loser. So they were probably telling him he rode good.

By the time he'd secured Rainbow and walked back to the tipi ring as dignified as he could manage, old Weeping Snakes and the she-male agent were seated on a medicine blanket in front of his lodge. The blanket was set diagonally, with one corner facing each of the main compass points. The black corner pointed north, the red corner pointed east and the white corner west, so naturally the blue corner was aimed south. Weeping Snakes had invited Miss Woodford to sit south of him, so Longarm sat down on the black corner, to have even more honor than their host according to most Ho-speaking bands. But Weeping Snakes just chuckled and said, "I wear red. I sit on red. I do this because the East has been given to me by Ometeotl. My people range farther east than any other Pan-Iti."

"That's what we wanted to talk to you about," said Longarm.

Weeping Snakes shook his head and said, "My daughter, here, has already told me about the Ome-Kiho, I mean two women. Forgive me. We were just speaking as real people and my head needs time to get all its Saltu words together."

"They don't have the two missing carnival girls, Longarm," Miss Woodford said. "They don't even know what happened to them. This is the first they've heard about the matter."

Longarm raised an eyebrow and looked straight at Weeping Snakes as he replied, "Do tell? Funny, but I got the distinct impression this band was hid out up here for *some* reason."

Weeping Snakes nodded. "There was a fight. We rode away to keep from having another war with you Saltu.

91

The last one we had was not a good fight. I knew when our greatest war leader, Buffalo Horn, was killed in the first real battle that you Saltu had the best teotl."

"Tea what?"

"Teotl is what the Lakota call Wakan and the Cheyenne call Manitou. The words do not come out right in your own tongue. It is not exactly Spirit. It is not exactly Magic. I don't know how to say Teotl in Saltu."

"Oh, you mean *Medicine*. I know *that* ain't it, neither, but it's the term most of us is agreed on. Can we get back to how come you and your band are holed up here? No offense, but I was risen by a different religion."

Weeping Snakes said, "I know. I think it was very cruel to nail that boy who hadn't done anything bad to a cross. I am not bad, either. I don't have any Saltu captives. None of my young men took any Saltu captives. None of them even took *hair* when the crazy Saltu attacked us at that tent show. You may search this camp all you like. Nobody will stop you. If you find any Saltu women or fresh scalps I will eat them raw and let you kill me. We have hidden here only to avoid more trouble. I sent for my Saltu daughter here because I want her to tell the Great White Father and his Blue Sleeves it was not our fault. We did not start the fight. Tell the Blue Sleeves you scout for it was not our fault."

Longarm nodded soberly and said, "I don't ride for the army no more. I'm sort of what you might call a Dog Soldier for Uncle Sam. I make sure his rules don't get broke by bad men, red or white. Tell me what really happened, and if it was someone else's fault I will tell the Blue Sleeves not to ride against you this evening."

Weeping Snakes did no such thing. He opened the front of his blanket to commence pounding his bony chest with a bony fist as he closed his eyes and started chanting in Ho, with Miss Woodford translating, sad-eyed, as he sang out slowly:

> "Where shall my soul dwell?
>   Where is my true home?
>     When can I stop wandering?
>       I am miserable. I am afflicted. So I lift my
>         voice,
>       In wailing,
>         But do the spirits listen?
>           Have they forgotten the old dream
>             songs?"

Miss Woodford was crying by the time he'd finished three more stanzas that sounded much the same to Longarm. The song had to have four stanzas anyway, because four was a good number to most Indians. For the same reasons three sounded right to whites, most likely.

When the old man had run out of dream-song words he stopped just as suddenly, switched back to matter-of-fact English, and said, "It was not the tent-show people who started the trouble, either. So why would we have taken women from them? The trouble was started by other Saltu who had come to the show to play the games and get drunk. I think the first man who threw a punch was a cowhand. He was young. He was drunk. He was loud. He said it was wrong for Anishinabeg to be there, even losing, and—"

"Anny what?" Longarm cut in, not wanting to miss any details.

Weeping Snakes said, "We are Ho, of the Pan-Iti-Nehmeh nation. Those you call Shoshone are Nihmih, not Nehmeh. Those you call Utes are No-Och-Nihwi and you call the Absaroke Crows."

"So which ones are Anny-whatevers?"

"All the people *you* call *Indians* for some reason are Anishinabeg. The cowhand said Indian, when he said we had no right to be there. But I think he really punched Running Elk because he wanted to punch me and my young man wouldn't let him."

"How come he wanted to punch you, then?"

"Because I was winning, of course. The tent-show people were good sports about it. Even *Saltu* who gamble for a living know it is woman-hearted to cry when one loses. But the young cowhand had lost money, much money, on the same wheel of fortune. So when I started winning he called me something . . . Let me see if I can remember. Oh, yes, he said I was shrill."

"You mean he accused you of being a *shill?*"

"Oh, yes, that was the word. What does it mean?"

"A shill is a gent who's in league with the gamblers, pretending to win so's dumber folk will bet. I know better than to ask you if the gamblers asked a full-blood right out to act as a shill. But there's more'n one way to get free labor without tedious discussion. The wheel-of-fortune operator could have been gulling everyone concerned. How much did they let you win the other night?"

The old man reached inside his blanket, took out a leather poke, and spilled the contents on the blanket between them. Longarm blinked hard at the twenty-dollar double-eagles mixed in with all those silver cartwheels and said, "Jesus Christ! Sorry, Miss Woodford, there's enough cold cash there to pay off a whole outfit after roundup! I take back what I suspicioned about them using you as a come-on, Weeping Snakes. You won too much off 'em for the tent show gents to be in on it with you on *purpose!* But let's study this some. In all fairness to the other suckers assembled, it just ain't *possible* to win that much off a wheel of fortune, honest. They don't *make* wheels of fortune that way!"

Weeping Snakes shrugged and began to put his small fortune back in the poke as he said, "I did not cheat. I have good Teotl. I have had good Teotl since I had my vision, atop the mountain, as I was praying to Ometeotl for guidance. It was a good vision. It has been coming true ever since I put down my war lance."

"It must have been, if you've been whipping professional tinhorns regularly despite the laws of chance and human crookedness! What did your Ommy-tea-total tell you, old son?"

"Do not mock the Great Double Medicine. He, she, or it controls the lightning, too. The Great Spirit told me that the Shining Times were over and that if I kept following the warpath I would only wind up bleaching with the buffalo bones, and poor old Buffalo Horn, under the uncaring gaze of Tona-Tiuh. You call him the sun. The Great Spirit said the only way to survive in the Fifth World you Saltu had taken over was to be strong in the Saltu way. To have *money*. Lots of money. Not the pittance the BIA offers Anishinabeg to act tame. The kind of money your big chiefs like Astor and Vanderbilt have. When a man has enough money, he can make even Saltu do anything he wants. I know this is true. The time some Saltu wanted our Kitlaztlan, even though the BIA said it was ours, they paid some judge with money and came in to dig holes in Tonantzin anyway! My Saltu daughter here can tell you this is true. She is not a bad agent, like the last one, who kept trying to sell our land out from under us."

The white girl raised a hand to quiet him as she explained to Longarm, "Kitlaztlan is what they call Fool's

Gold Valley. Tonantzin is their Mother Earth. I've explained those prospectors found no color and that the crook who gave them the permit to file a claim on Indian land hasn't been with the BIA since the Hayes reform administration heard about it. But we still can't get him to go back there and stay put."

Weeping Snakes frowned at her and said, "Hear me, Kitlaztlan is not a damned *reservation!* It is our own Starry Land, found by us and held by us before you Saltu ever saw it!"

Longarm nodded. "Agreed. You can't hardly get a better deal off the BIA than to be assigned your home range as your official reservation. So what are we arguing about?"

The medicine man snorted in disgust and said, "You certainly are dumb for a man who ducks bullets so good, Longarm. We don't want the beautiful meadows and campus flats of Kitlaztlan as a *reservation*. We want to *own* it!"

"Ain't we talking about the same thing, Weeping Snakes?"

"Of course not. Did the Lakota really own their Black Hills when the government gave it to them, forever, as a reservation?"

Longarm didn't answer.

Weeping Snakes sneered. "Hear me, the Lakota were allowed to keep the Black Hills until white trespassers found gold on Indian land. When the Lakota tried to chase them away, the thieving Saltu called on the Blue Sleeves to protect them, and the Blue Sleeves did! The Great White Father used what happened next, at Little Bighorn, as an excuse to take the Black Hills back from the Lakota. Do you deny this, Longarm?"

"Well, mistakes was made on both sides. But I won't

argue your main thrust. Getting back to Fool's Gold Valley, though, it's been trespassed and found wanting in color. So I doubt anyone else will ever try to take it away from you no matter *who* wins the next election."

"That's another crazy thing you Saltu do," the old man complained. "Every four years you choose new chiefs. Four is a good number. But it's still bad for *us!* Hear me, when we make a treaty with you we expect you to keep it. But what good is a treaty when four years later, new chiefs say they never signed it and don't have to do what the old chiefs agreed to?"

Longarm sighed wearily and said, "I ain't got no easy answers, Weeping Snakes. Our notions of government ain't perfect, but they ain't near as bad as the way other governments in other parts is set up. If you was under the Tsar of All the Russias you'd be in even a worse fix, I'll vow. Meanwhile, we are talking about a reserve for you and, while you say you admire it a lot, you still don't *want* it? You sure are one contrary old son of a . . . never mind. Ladies present."

The lady present said, "I understand what they want, Longarm. We've talked about it before. The Bannock want to buy the land outright, as their own, free and simple, and sort of fire me."

Weeping Snakes nodded and told Longarm, "My Saltu daughter is smarter than you, even if she is a Kaho, a not-man. Any man with enough money is allowed to buy land from your Land Office. When he does they give him a Saltu deed, saying the land is the land of him and his children forever. True?"

"Well, as long as somebody pays taxes on it, anyway. But you sure are going about this the hard way, Weeping Snakes. I ain't even sure an Indian is allowed to own land free and simple, though, since they've allowed a

97

mess of immigrants who don't even talk English to file homestead claims since the War, it seems only fair. But the Land Office will charge you plenty for the acreage we're talking about, and the land tax you'd wind up paying after that would be more'n you can get off the BIA as a tribal allowance without going to so much trouble."

"I will always have money. I have good teotl, and your kind will always gamble."

"Oh, Lord, even a medicine man has to know a winning streak can't last forever, Weeping Snakes! I don't know how in thunder you've got so far ahead of the game. But my *own* visions tell me your luck has to run out in time and, meantime, you're being mighty picky about land titles to land nobody's trying to take away from you in the first place. So what say you just lead your folk over where they belong so Miss Woodford, here, can set up a proper station for you?"

"Hear me. We don't want a trading post. We don't want a schoolhouse. We don't want even good-hearted Saltu telling us when to get up and when to go to bed. We are Pan-Iti. We are Ho. We are the Real Men. We will live on our own land, free. Or we will wander free as we can manage until somebody kills us. I have spoken!"

Miss Woodford started to say something soothing to the old man. But Longarm pulled her up with him, muttering, "He just told you he's spoken, ma'am. We was talking in circles with him towards the end in any case. Come on. We'd best get back to civilization and get the army to act civilized for now."

She let him lead her away as the old medicine man ducked back inside his tipi. But she asked, "If the Bannock don't have those captive carnival girls, who do you think could have carried them off, Longarm?"

"Don't know. Ain't fixing to find out *here*. By the way, my closer associates call me Custis. I can't help it. It's what they named me."

She laughed and said, "My first name's Irene. I'm not sure how close I want to associate with you, though. So let go my arm, hear?"

# Chapter 9

As they rode into the army post the colonel and his lady were talking to the old scout, Beaver, on the veranda of the CO's quarters. Beaver's paint pony was tethered to a hitching rail out front, and that was where Longarm and Irene Woodford left theirs. Longarm tied up both their mounts as Irene clumped and jingled up the veranda steps. The motherly but not bad-looking old gal who was wedded to the colonel invited her inside to freshen up. But Irene wanted to jaw with the colonel first, and as Longarm joined them she'd already told them that Weeping Snakes didn't have the two missing white gals.

Longarm was braced for an argument. It was hard to get promoted in an Indian-fighting army without fighting Indians. But the CO just nodded and said Beaver had just told him much the same.

Beaver spat, over the rail to be polite, and went on, "Yep, I was out there earlier. Scouted the camp some afore I made my move, then rid in to powwow with the old buzzard, the same as you all."

Longarm frowned and started to ask a dumb question. But since neither he nor Irene had asked about any other visitors and Indians seldom answered questions they weren't asked, it made sense.

He asked Beaver, "Did you know your pony's missing a nail in his left kind shoe?" Beaver said he hadn't noticed. Then he dropped down off the veranda, moved around to the rear of his paint, and had a look before he called up, "He sure is, Longarm. But how did you know? Nobody has eyes *that* good!"

Longarm replied, "I misread sign, up to Kate's Crossing. Your mount left some clear prints when you scouted that railroad car and then rode on. Were you the one who opened the door?"

Beaver shook his head as he rejoined them. "Nope. It were wide open as I rid into the ghost town. I wondered what it was doing there, so I had a look-see. I still don't know why the railroad seen fit to park a car out in the middle of nowheres. There was a hole chopped in the bottom of her, too. The Indians say *they* never done it."

"They didn't," said Longarm, dropping it there to avoid a long, tedious tale with some parts he didn't want to repeat in front of the two ladies.

The colonel didn't seem interested in empty boxcars. He said, "Well, if the Bannock don't have any white captives, it seems a waste of time to sound Boots-and-Saddles this evening. It's starting to look more like a case for you civilian lawmen, Longarm. Unless they just ran off to join the circus, some *white* men must have abducted them!"

Longarm nodded. "They'd *already* run off to join a circus, or a traveling tent show, anyway. After I tend some other chores I'll see if I can catch up with the tent show and at least find out who I'm looking for. Show folk like to have their pictures taken, and it hardly seems likely the kidnappers carried off their luggage as well. The most important point is that we're talking about a plain old criminal felony, not an Indian raid."

The colonel nodded and said, "I *said* the war's over for now. But unless someone can get those Bannock to light somewhere and stay put, it's only a question of time."

He turned to Irene. "Isn't it possible to get the BIA to issue them a reserve some other place if they're so dead set against returning to Fool's Gold Valley, Miss Woodford?"

"Most of the Bitterroot range is federal property," Irene said. "We could designate almost any part of it as an Indian reservation. But Weeping Snakes doesn't seem to want to settle down for good anywhere but that particular valley, sir."

Longarm could see she was about to repeat the whole fool talk with Weeping Snakes, and he'd found it sort of tedious the first time around. So he excused himself and walked down the line to the post armory. He went inside, showed his badge and ID to the ordinance sergeant, and said, "I need a saddle gun. I'll sign for it. I need the carbine more than I need an argument, Sarge."

The noncom shrugged and said, "I never argue with gents coming in from officer country. We got Springfield conversions and Spencer repeaters. We ain't got nothing better. So name your pleasure."

Longarm grimaced. "Never mind. I can likely pick up a Winchester in town. I see now why your colonel is so reasonable about Indians."

The ordinance sergeant sighed. "Look at her this way,"

he said. "At the rate we're going, the army can hold an antique sale any day now and make a bundle. It's been seriously said amongst the troops that the War Department is out to avoid paying pensions by making it impossible for any man in this man's army to survive his full ten hitches."

Longarm told him to cheer up, since the price of beef had risen and most outfits were paying a dollar a day for a man who could ride at all. Then he went back to see if Irene Woodford was ready to ride back to town yet.

She wasn't. The colonel was alone with Beaver on the veranda. He said the little lady was having tea inside with his wife and that when she was through sipping the same she meant to send some wires to the BIA over the army wire out here. Longarm consulted his watch and opined, "I ain't got that much time to spare, rude as riding off on her might seem."

The colonel said he didn't doubt she'd find an officer or more willing to escort her safely back to town. Longarm didn't doubt it either. Good-looking gals got escorted all over creation whether they wanted to be or not. So he said in that case he'd just escort himself into town, and they shook on it.

The high country the Indians called the Shining Mountains and the whites the Rockies was laid out more complicated than one might suspect, looking at a map. So though the neat dotted line that stood for the Continental Divide followed the crests of the Bitterroots to the south, it snaked across suspiciously low ridges toward Helena to follow another range entirely up to Canada, putting the parklike valley, the fort, and the town named after it officially on the western slope of the Rockies, even though the Bitterroots to the west still looked high. Like most mountain parks, the valley itself was wide and more like rolling prairie than alpine. But there were clumps of lodgepole pine and cottonwoods or aspens scattered along the trail, depending on how wet the soil was under an otherwise evenly sun-baked sod. Longarm had just ridden around a twist in the trail through an aspen glade when Rainbow shied at something and bucked halfway to the sky.

This time Longarm didn't try to stay aboard, for he'd heard the whipcrack of a high-powered rifle·just as Rainbow lifted him halfway to the treetops. He rolled out of the saddle as Rainbow dropped back down, farther than usual, in a tangled heap of screaming horseflesh.

Longarm landed with his legs more solid, but dropped to the dust behind Rainbow as another rifle round hummed over him, drawing his own .44 as he did so, and cussing himself for not accepting that old Spencer repeater back at the post. Any kind of rifle was better than a revolver when some son of a bitch was peppering you at rifle range.

Rainbow made a lousy fort, thrashing his big hooves and carrying on like that, so Longarm shot him in the head. A mount that had taken a high-powered round well into the guts was no use to anyone and likely in some discomfort. As the poor brute went limp, Longarm removed his Stetson and raised it just above the flank of the dead gelding on the barrel of his .44. The bushwhacker hidden in the aspens blew it way down the trail behind Longarm's boot heels, so Longarm knew he was still there, and still serious.

Longarm looked around for a graceful exit. There didn't seem to be one. The town was close, just around the next bend, but Longarm didn't think he could outrun a bullet across the open stretch that way. There was nothing but short-grass and a few granite rocks even smaller than the corpse of Rainbow to either side. The son of a bitch with the rifle had all the decent cover there was around here.

On the other hand, to gun a man forted behind a horse the rascal would have to either charge across open ground head-on, or try to flank Longarm with the ground as open to left and right. So things could have been worse. Longarm thought, *Well, it ain't all that hot, and the sun ball will go down long before you can die of hunger and thirst, old son. So just sit tight and see how long a siege the son of a bitch aims to make of it.*

He called out tauntingly, "Hey, popgun? You want to finish this sooner, man to man? You got the range on me. How come you ain't got the hair on your chest to come out and fight?"

No answer.

"You're fixing to get eaten alive by ticks in them aspens, pilgrim! Show *yourself* and I'll show *me,* you yellow-livered gun punk!"

That didn't work, either. Longarm fished out a cheroot and lit it, since he could see he had time for a smoke. He'd smoked the cheroot more than halfway down when he heard hoofbeats on the trail behind him and swung his gun muzzle that way. Then a couple of cowhands rounded the bend, saw what was pointing at them from the trail ahead, and reined in.

Longarm called out, "I'm law. There's a gent who ain't in yonder aspen glade, with a high-powered rifle. Ride back to town and get me some backup here, will you?"

They did no such thing, being young and foolish. They both let out war whoops, drew their own guns, and split up to circle the downed deputy from either side, riding at the clump of aspen from both flanks and shooting into the close-packed saplings as they rode.

Had the rifleman still been there, he'd have surely gotten one or both of them. But he didn't. So Longarm knew he'd ridden out the far side. As he got to his feet, the young hands rode back to him, both grinning like the fools they'd just proved themselves. One of them asked Longarm what was going on.

"Don't never do such a fool thing again, boys," Longarm said. "Some son of a bitch just shot my mount, aiming at the small of my back, most likely, and I'm much obliged to you both for clearing the matter up so crazy. I was afraid I'd be stuck here longer."

The other young hand spat and said, "Shit, a man who tries to gun another in the back, from cover, ain't nobody the Slash Bar W has to fear. That's who we rides for, the Slash Bar W. I'm Slim Ferris and this here ugly runt is Ozark Owens. That rascal surely put your mount on the ground for keeps, lawman. How do you figure to get into town now?"

"The walk won't kill me, even if it is at least a quarter of a mile or more. If you boys are headed that way, I'd sure like to buy you that drink I owe you."

Slim said, "We can't take you up on it now. We ain't supposed to be this fur south as it is."

Ozark winked. "We're supposed to be looking for strays. But we snuck into town to get laid. Got laid good, too. They got new talent at the parlor house across from the Grasshopper. Ask for Miss Tillie if you likes French loving. She ain't French by birth, but she sure has studied the lingo, if you know what I means."

Slim snorted. "Hell, that blonde, Sunshine Sal, is too good a screwer to waste a load in her *French!* Come on, Ozark. We got to git back to work. It's been nice meeting you, lawman. Take my advice about women when you get to town. Sunshine Sal will treat you right for a dollar, hear?"

Longarm thanked them for coming to his assistance and dropped to one knee to salvage the saddle and bridle, at least, for now. The two young hands had ridden off by the time he was limping on to town with the gear on his left shoulder and the .44 still in his right fist, just in case. His right knee hurt some from the way he'd parted company with the late Rainbow. But as he trudged on it started feeling better and he was walking almost good as new by the time he got into town and put the gun away.

It was now past high noon and hot outside. He didn't meet many folk on the walks as he clumped to the livery. He draped the army bridle and the saddle with his coat lashed to it over a stall rail and told the hostler, "I'll be back directly, and when I get here, I'll want a horse. I mean one for a man to ride, not a nag meant for women and children to go to church on. The one I was just on lies dead on the trail just outside of town. What do you reckon we ought to do about it?"

The hostler said, "For one thing, we'll require a considerable deposit afore we let you ride one of *our* horses! How'd you manage to kill your pony, mister?"

"I ain't a mister. I'm a deputy U. S. marshal. I had to shoot my army mount because some other bastard shot him first. Don't worry about the deposit. I'm on an expense account. The buckskin shot out from under me figures to start stinking soon, in this hot sun."

The hostler said he knew a hide skinner down the way who'd likely clean up the mess if Longarm didn't want too much for the hide. Longarm said the skinner was welcome to it as long as he made sure the trail was clear. Then he turned away and went to the Western Union again to bring Billy Vail up to date on the odd way this case seemed to be going.

Not knowing who had just tried to gun him, he didn't hazard a guess about it in the wire he sent his boss. He strode over to the nearby railroad yards to check up on the present whereabouts of the one enemy he knew he had for a fact in these parts.

But the Emperor Edwards just wouldn't fit as the bushwhacker. The dispatcher in the freight office said he knew the Emperor, and agreed he was a mean son of a bitch, but added that unless he'd fallen out of his caboose along the way he'd be in Spokane right now, shacked up with a gal he knew there as he waited for a train to brake back this way. The dispatcher said, "He should be coming through here just after midnight if you have to see him."

Longarm frowned and answered, "Ain't sure I *has* to see him, but I surely *wants* to if I ain't got more ominous fish to fry. Tell me something, pard. Could the bastard have been here in Fort Missoula at least a few hours after coming in with that train last night?"

The dispatcher shook his head and said, "Not hardly. They only stayed here long enough to uncouple and re-dispatch a dozen or so cars. Then they put her back together and headed on up the line. I reckon Edwards would have had time to sneak a drink or two. But had he drunk *three* he'd have surely been left ahint. He wasn't, though, for he wired they was on schedule when they stopped at Clark's Junction to jerk water less'n two hours after they left here. The old Emperor will be raking another freight back this way after laying over in Spokane a spell. But that's where you'll find him right *now*, Deputy."

Longarm thanked the dispatcher and headed back to the main street, frowning mighty puzzled. He was running low on suspects, even though he knew for a fact that *some* damned somebody in these parts didn't like him any more than the surly brakeman had. But the Indians had no reason to be sore at him and, even if they were, a Bannock out to bushwhack him would have had a better crack at his back out in the woods near the ghost town.

The army had no reasons to gun him, even had the regulations said they could. The BIA had asked for his help in the first place, and the only BIA agent within miles had been sipping tea when Rainbow was murdered. That left ... Yeah, the rascal who'd opened that boxcar door for whatever reason. Or was he lining up unrelated facts to draw a fool pattern that wasn't really there?

Indian kids exploring the ghost town could have busted the seal and opened the car door just because kids did things like that. It couldn't have been the Emperor Edwards, since he was long gone. It couldn't have been a curious railroad worker, since the railroad didn't seem to know the car had been routed there. But how *had* the boxcar wound up on that deserted siding? It hadn't just rolled itself up an abandoned spur from the main line.

He started to turn back. But he decided not to bother. He'd heard the treacherous brakeman telling someone else to dispatch the car to Kate's Crossing, and the other gent had sounded dumb and innocent. He'd likely been a switch-engine driver or something. Tracking him down would be easy enough, but what could the gent tell him that he didn't already know? It might be more interesting to say nothing and see who did scout up that abandoned car a second time, when the nasty brakeman came through again.

He went to the hotel to see if Jemima had got off all right.

She had. The day clerk stared at Longarm sort of

thoughtfully as he confirmed that a young gal in a new dress had indeed come down earlier from rooms hired by a couple of gents the night before. But Longarm saw no need to explain, since the room rents had run out and he didn't aim to check in again, with or without a hobo of either sex.

He went to the depot, made sure Jemima had caught the southbound passenger combo that had left hours ago, and muttered, "Hell, she had no reason to gun me, anyway." Then, having run out of notions for now, and not having had a drink for some time, he went back to the Grasshopper for some needled beer.

It being a weekday during worktime, the saloon was empty as well as dark and restful. Longarm carried his schooner to a table and sat down to ponder.

A schooner later, he was just as bemused about the strange goings-on in these parts, but feeling less morose and sweaty, at least. Then he heard his name called from somewhere outside and got up to go to the doorway. The clerk from the Western Union was standing in the street, waving a telegram as he yelled, "This just came in for you, urgent, Deputy Long!"

Longarm stepped out and took the message, inviting the clerk in for a drink at the same time. The clerk said Western Union wouldn't let him drink on duty, and made Longarm sign for the special wire. Longarm carried it back in and read it as he sat there sipping suds.

Vail had wired that since the Indian trouble seemed to have been a false alarm and he'd talked as much sense to Weeping Snakes as the law allowed, all was forgiven and he was to get his [deleted by Western Union] back to Denver as there were more important saucepans on the stove.

Longarm shrugged, balled the wire up, and tossed it

110

across the saloon at a spittoon by the bar rail. It bounced out, but he counted it as on target anyway. There was lots of other trash mixed with the sawdust to be swept up some day.

The tough old gal called Red Robin came out from the back to sit down beside him, saying, "I heard someone call your name just now. It woke me from a wet dream."

He chuckled and said, "I noticed." Red Robin was only wearing a red kimono, half open, with nothing on under it. He added, "I like your outfit. It matches your hair. The hair on your head, leastways."

Red Robin smiled roguishly and replied, "I got other bottles aside from the one my henna rinse comes in, in my quarters. Are you still drinking Maryland rye, Custis?"

"Every chance I get. But ain't it a mite early for drinking?"

She said, "Last night you said it was too *late*. What's got into you, honey? I looked in the mirror just now and I'll be switched if I've busted out in spots or grown a harelip since the last time we got somewhat closer down Texas way. Have you got another gal here in Montana Territory, you brute?"

He told her, truthfully enough, "Not right now. I had made plans to ride down to Fool's Gold Valley and see what all the fuss was about, or the other way, to catch up with a tent show and see if they're still missing those two carnival gals. But my boss just wired me to come on home, and I just don't know what to do. The BIA's dispute with the Bannock seems more tedious than unlawful, and while kidnapping can't be constitutional, it's still a local affair until said gals get taken across a state or territorial line."

111

Red Robin said, "It's not seemly for me to be setting here so exposed, off duty, should other customers come in. What say we go to my place and I'll help you study on your next move, honey."

That sounded fair. There wouldn't be another train south for a spell in any case, and he thought it might be more fun to ride south late with the Emperor Edwards, in any case. So he drained his schooner and got up to follow Red Robin out the back way.

She led him next door, down the alley, and up an outside stairway like the one running up to Irene Woodford's BIA office. As they got inside he felt sure the other gal's office had to be more sedate. Red Robin traveled too much to paint her walls. But she'd hung red velvet drapes over the windows and around the hired four-poster. The bedspread was red velvet, too, and when she turned the covers down he saw her sheets were red satin. She sure like red. It was sort of a shame the wallpaper that came with the place was orange and purple paisley. Red Robin dropped her red kimono atop the bedspread rolled out of the way and strode bare-ass to the dressing table she'd set up as a sort of bar, asking, "Want your rye with branch water or just the way she comes?"

He started shucking his own duds as he replied, as matter-of-factly, "I'd best not drink no more right now. I've already had two needled beers, and I don't like to stagger in such pretty mixed company."

She laughed, helped herself to a healthy swig from the bottle, and said, "It don't matter if *I* fall down, since I figure to spend most of the time on the bottom in any case." Then she put down the bottle, turned around, and ran at him to leap high in the air and lock her naked arms and legs around him as they crashed back across the bed together.

He protested that wasn't fair, since he was only half naked. But Red Robin hauled his pants halfway down and spitted herself on his love stake while it was still rising to the occasion. It rose inside her indeed, once Red Robin's skilled interior had the matter firmly in hand. He protested, "Let me get my goddamn boots and britches all the way off, honey!"

But she hissed, "Later! I'm so hot it's sheer painsome! You said you were coming back last night, you bastard! Who did you spend the rest of the night with instead?"

"I cannot tell a lie. I was shacked up with a hobo calt Jim. We met riding the rails together, and—"

But she cut in, "Never mind! It don't matter where you were last night, for I can tell you're as hard up as me, you sweet loving thing!"

It was a hell of a time for a she-male to climax and fall weak and limp on a man. Longarm rolled her over on her back without taking it out and, though his pants about his booted ankles felt sort of silly, he had a mighty nice angle of attack with his feet on the rug and Red Robin's hips on the edge of the mattress like that. So that was how he came in her the first time, hard. Then he dismounted to sit bare-ass beside her as he finished taking off his boots and pants, growling, "So much for foreplay. Let's get down to *screwing*, little darling!"

She gasped weakly, "Can we take a little breather first? I'm out of practice and I'd forgotten how impossible you're hung."

He just laughed, plumped up a red satin pillow to wedge under her plush hips, and got back aboard to do it right as Red Robin started to protest, then moaned in pleasure and started moving her upthrust pelvis in time with his thrusts. This time they came at the same time and she said, "Oh, that was so lovely, Custis. Why is it we seem to screw so good together? We ain't done it

113

often enough to call it love, but it do feel *good!*"

He nuzzled her bare throat as he answered with a contented sigh, "It's always better once two bodies get used to one another's ways. Knowing when you're about to jump the fence, I can post in the saddle better to take the jump *with* you, see?"

"Oh, yes, keep moving it gentle in me like that. My God, to think I almost shot you that time down in Texas. Of course I had no way of knowing, then, what a crime I'd be committing against all womankind! You're just joshing when you say you like my screwing best, right?"

"Nope," he replied, truthfully enough for the time and place. "After I've made love to a pretty little thing like you more than once, I do seem to get better at it. *You're* screwing better now than you did that first time I disarmed you down in Texas. Reckon you don't feel as distracted, now that you know I ain't out to arrest you after all."

She laughed and started moving under him faster, but being a she-male and therefore curious enough for any dozen cats, Red Robin had to go and almost break the spell by saying, "If you're so sure that sex improves with experience, you surely must have other old friends you do this to now and again, right?"

He did. He was sort of looking forward to the widow woman on Sherman Avenue again. But he told Red Robin, "I ain't got nobody but you, stale *or* fresh, lined up here in Montana Territory. I did hear there's two new fancy gals working in the parlor house across the way. But I'm too delicate-natured to mess with outright whores."

She sighed. "Oh, you treats a gal so romantical, Custis. I thank you for not calling me a whore, an *outright* whore, leastways."

He started moving in her faster as he soothed, "Hush, you ain't no whore. You're a piano player. There's a big difference, even if you do meet lots of the same customers."

"Oh, you're so understanding, lover man! So many men take my late hours and henna rinse the wrong way. But you know I never do this sort of thing for *money*, don't you?"

"Sure, like me, you like to screw too much to make a business out of it. Can we talk about it some more later? Right now I'm fixing to come in you some more."

She answered with a moan of passion and raised her legs to lock her ankles around the nape of Longarm's neck as he pounded her to glory with him. She sure looked handsome with the sunlight filtering through red drapes to make her look like she was blushing all over. It even made the hair between her thighs look sort of red as he watched his shaft slide in and out of her until they suddenly collapsed in one big ball of pulsating, protracted orgasm.

When they pulled their brains back down from heaven, Red Robin sighed, "I'm sorry. I know it sounds dumb. But right now I surely love you, Custis, and it don't seem right to love a man and not tell him."

He could see she was feeling romantic and mushy, and he knew what she wanted him to say in return. She was right. It was dumb. But he kissed her and almost meant it when he replied, "Right now I feel sort of loving, too. It wouldn't be natural to feel any other way in bed with such a sweet little gal. But you understand, a man who packs a badge for a living has no business promising anything *more* to any gal, even at times like these."

"I ain't proposing marriage, you fool. I just thought a proper gent ought to at least tell a gal he loves her whilst he's fucking her, God damn it!"

He laughed and said, "Oh, hell, I loves you more'n any other gal in sight right now. Satisfied?"

"Not hardly. Can't you get it in any deeper, darling?"

He could and he did, and the next time she came, she came so hard it knocked her out. Or at least she said she wanted to sleep some before they did it again. So he cuddled her henna-rinsed head on his shoulder and smoked a cheroot as Red Robin closed her eyes and started snoring softly. He wondered why he wasn't the least bit sleepy. His body felt tired enough. It was sort of tedious, just lying here listening to her snore while any number of more interesting things could be going on in the broad daylight outside. So when he'd finished his smoke he rolled her head off his shoulder gently, trying not to wake Red Robin up.

He didn't. She rolled over with her hourglassed backside to him, murmuring, "Not again, George. Let me sleep, you horny thing."

He smiled crookedly as he eased out the far side, wondering who George might be, and what business it could be of his in any case. For he and Robin hadn't exchanged any serious vows that time in Texas, and he'd been with lots of gals nobody called Red Robin since then.

# Chapter 10

He tried not to let it annoy him as he quietly got dressed again in the ruby gloom of Red Robin's room. He knew it wasn't fair for any man to expect all the gals he laid to remain true to him between times. But that was another simple fact of nature, too. Every man and doubtless every woman dreamed of a love life that was just plain impossible. He knew his old semi-steady lady, the widow woman on Sherman Avenue, fooled about when he was out of town like this. Knew she'd demand to know, when he got back, whether he'd been true to *her* this time, too. Naturally he'd say he had, and he'd take her word, too. For all great lovers pined for a world where they got to screw around all they liked with a mess of lovers who were true to them alone.

He eased to his feet, put on his hat, and let himself out sneaky as, on the bed across the room, Red Robin moaned in her sleep, "Not that way, Pete! You know I don't like it that way, damn it!"

He shut the door before she could get around to Tom, Dick, or Harry. He knew she didn't really mess around with as many men as some thought a saloon piano player should, but... *Pete,* too? Who the hell was Pete, and what right did a man who'd never met him have to ball his fist up so? Whoever Pete was, he hadn't done anything *George* hadn't done, right?

Longarm, who'd just done as much or more, moved down to the alley and followed it to a gap between buildings. As he stepped back out on the street he saw Beaver and another scout who looked more Indian reining in in front of the saloon where he'd been drinking alone earlier. Beaver spotted Longarm and waved. Longarm waved back. Then he turned away and headed for the livery. He could tell the army about Rainbow later. For a man paid to scout, Beaver sure spent a lot of time drinking during business hours.

At the livery they told him he could hire a black mare with a star blaze if he put down a fifty-dollar deposit. He said the fool mare wasn't worth no fifty dollars dead or alive, and in the end they settled on twenty. As he rode out aboard her, he wondered if the Justice Department had still been skinned. Her name was Blaze, of course, but it should have been Snail or Stubborn. She had nice lines for a scrub pony, but when he tried to heel her into a lope she just stopped dead in the trail and turned her barrel head back to shoot a reproachful look at him.

He growled, "That's what they generally give you to ride at a stable—a stable horse." He heeled her harder and said, "If it please your majesty, could we at least make it to the hardware store on the corner before you lay your head on my shoulder and start snoring?"

Blaze moved on with injured dignity and when he

reined in a few yards down the drag she lowered her head, as if exhausted, to drool at the dust between her front hooves. He dismounted and had to crank her fool head up to tether her in front of the hardware store. He went in and told the pimple-faced kid behind the counter he needed a Winchester and a couple of boxes of .44-40s. The clerk said they had the ammo, but that the only repeater they had for sale chambered to take the same was a Henry.

Longarm muttered, "This just ain't my day, save for romance, I reckon. All right, at least a Henry has a *Spencer* beat! Don't wrap it up. I'll just shoot it as I carry it home."

He carried his purchases back outside. He put the spare ammo in the pockets of the coat lashed to the saddle, save for a fistful in his pants. The army saddle didn't have a carbine boot, but the Henry had a carrying ring welded to the blank side of its action. So he lashed it with a slip knot to one of the brass loops army saddles had stuck all over them and let it hang straight down with its stock in line with the off-side cantle. He moved around to the near-side, unhitching as he circled, and mounted up. The Henry rode about right, with its stock just behind his right hip. He adjusted the cross-draw .44 more comfortably on his left hip. Then he lit another cheroot and told Blaze, "If it ain't too big a bother, I'd like to go someplace now, Sleeping Beauty."

Blaze just stood there, trying to get her head back down.

"All right," he said. "I can see you need medication." He dismounted, went back in the hardware store, and said, "I need some turpentine. Not a whole can. Just a dab on this here kerchief. How much?"

The clerk said there would be no charge for a man

who'd just bought a whole rifle without arguing price all that much. A few seconds later Longarm had gone back out, remounted, and twisted in the saddle to reach back with both hands as he held the reins in his teeth. He yanked the mare's tail up with one. That got her moving some. But not half as much as she moved once he'd dabbed her ass with turpentine.

Blaze almost left Longarm behind as she streaked north out of town in a dead run, screaming like a banshee and bucking some along the way, as she tried to cool her ass by waving it in the breeze. But he'd suspicioned she might do something like that. So he just held on with his legs and let her have her head, tucking the kerchief in a hip pocket as the stock of the Henry spanked his own behind. He reached down and grabbed the carbine to steady it with his free hand, cussing the army for not providing a proper saddle-gun boot and cussing himself for having left Denver in such a hurry. But as the mare settled down to a more sedate lope he forgave himself, at least. For had he not run right for that freight without going home for his field gear, he might never have met up with poor little Jemima, and had the Emperor Edwards met her alone, there was no telling what might have happened to her.

He thought some more about that as he rode Blaze along the now deserted trail. He knew he was missing a piece of the puzzle every time he thought about that freight car. It seemed odd enough that the bully had routed it out to that ghost town at Kate's Crossing, not far from the Indian camp. It seemed odder still that the Emperor had taken such a chance at all. Brakemen were paid to be tough, but he'd met few who went in for premeditated murder.

The dirty trick wouldn't wash as just a dirty trick. No

matter how mad he'd made the Emperor feel by knocking him gently on his ass in front of his fellow railroaders, the Emperor had to know the rep of the man he was dealing with. If he hadn't, why had he passed up a chance for a fair fight, with him holding a wrench and backed by his yard bulls?

"We wasn't supposed to get out of that car alive," Longarm told his mount. "He wasn't counting on us dying of thirst locked up in her, either. Had we not got out, we'd *still* be alive up at Kate's Crossing, no matter how uncomfortable, and he must have known that someone was likely to come along and unlock that door sooner or later. So, yeah, he had somebody waiting there by that siding to let us out in the dawn's early light and gun us as we came out, still confused. But who? I never knocked but one brakeman on his ass, and the others didn't seem to really admire him all that much. Surely not enough to murder a U. S. deputy for him, leastways! Killing feds is too serious a notion even to consider, unless there's a mighty serious and likely profitable motive."

Blaze had no answers for him. She'd slowed to a mile-eating trot he allowed would do. But when they came to a creek ford across the trail, the fool horse sat down in the cold water like a dog, rubbing her behind on a mossy boulder. He said, "I'm getting my boots wet, stupid. So I'm saying it once. I ain't interested in sitting here in this creek with you all day. We got a tent show to catch up with, and if they've got *elephants* pulling their wagons they're still making better time than you and me!"

He pulled out the turpentine-scented kerchief and waved it as far forward as he could reach without dismounting in the middle of a creek. She got the message. If horses could have talked, she'd have doubtless told him she didn't want to argue with him any more. She leaped out of the creek as if it was running with hot brimstone and, after that, he saw he wasn't going to have any more nonsense about who as in charge. Horses were a lot like kids. A grown-up just had to be a mite firm with them when they acted bratty.

They rode on till they came to a fork in the trail. Longarm reined in to stare morosely down at the churned-up dust, muttering, "Damn, no signpost and, even if there was, no way you can tell from here which way that infernal tent show might have gone."

There were wagon tracks, lots of them, leading up both trails, along with the hoofmarks of many a horse and even more unshod cows.

He studied for elephant sign, camel sign, *some* damned sign that might read tent show. But if the rascals had passed this way at all, they were using more sensible critters to pull their wagons. He was about to flip a coin when he heard his name called out behind him and turned in the saddle to see old Beaver coming at him at a lope. The scout reined in and said, "They said you'd rid out this way, Longarm. Where are you headed?"

Longarm pointed north with his chin. "After that tent show, if I could only figure out which way it went. Have you any notion, Beaver?"

Beaver grinned. "Sure. It's no secret their next stop is Freightown. We got some fair riding ahead of us if we mean to get there before sundown, though. It's a good fifteen miles or more."

"Do tell? Which fork, and how come *you're* on your way there as well, Beaver?"

"Just heard Weeping Snakes meant to pay it yet another visit. With any luck, we might catch up with him on the trail afore he gets there."

"Freightown a tough town for Indians to visit?"

Beaver spat. "Tough town for *anyone* to visit. Railroad marshaling yards and repair sheds. Section hands stationed there as well. Do I really have to draw you a picture?"

"Not hardly. Railroad towns ain't safe for anyone after dark, and lots of track walkers has been scalped by Indians, Bannock or not. How'd you find out Weeping Snakes was on another gambling spree?"

"That Delaware scout you seen me back in town with just now seen the old rascal ride out with a mess of his braves, and they was too gussied up to be hunting elk. That's what I was trying to tell you when you turnt your back on me so proud. I had to report it in to the colonel and jaw with him some afore I could join you in your quest for whatever. What are we questing, Longarm?"

Longarm shrugged and said, "Ain't sure I'm not on another fool's errand, but I like to have all the details down pat when I hand in my official report. I just got orders to return to Denver, but I know my boss will twit me if I leave any names out. So I mean to at least get the names and, if possible, some pictures of them missing carnival gals."

Beaver spat downwind, polite, and said, "Hell, *I* can tell you *that* much. They was named Edith and, let's see, Joy, that was her name. They was last seed near the end of the fairway when the light got confusing. I doubts anyone will ever find 'em, now."

"Do tell? What do you reckon happened to 'em, Beaver?"

"If the Bannock didn't take 'em, and the tent show ain't got 'em, it adds up to a Rape of the Sabine Women, engineered by Romans riding for some spread around here. They *hang* men for rape in Montana Territory. So once the old boys who grabbed them had time to sober some, they likely dropped 'em down any number of mine shafts. These hills are Swiss-cheesed with try holes from the gold-rush days, and did a man toss a barrel or so worth of loose tailings down after a body or more—"

"Finding body one would be a bitch," Longarm cut in. "I know of a gent who lay at the bottom of a Leadville try hole a good long time before some gents with no place better to try found his bones. And he'd just fallen in all by his fool self and lay on the bottom uncovered. I hope you're wrong about them missing gals. But if they was really kidnapped, it do seem unlikely they'll ever turn up in the Bitterroots, dead or alive."

They rode on for a time in silence. They passed through a big burn Beaver said had been started by careless greenhorns prospecting for gold. The charred trunks of trees all around gave mute evidence they hadn't known how to bury a campfire right before moving on. The scorched earth between the upright charcoal timbers was barely starting to heal with fireweed and, here and there, the sprout of a lodgepole pine or aspen. Longarm asked if the fools had found any color after burning down a few square miles of forest. Beaver shook his head and said, "Ain't no gold in these here hills to be found, no matter how many greenhorns look. That's likely why the Montana mining towns are off to the southeast a good eighty or ninety miles from here. They found a little color further north in the Bitterroots, where the bedrock crops closer to the surface. But even up thataway they ain't taking out all that much these days."

Longarm nodded. "I've been down in some hardrock mines. Been in the Mother Lode country out California way, too. The rocks I've seen around here, so far, don't look at all the same. But let's talk about Fool's Gold

Valley, or Kitlaztlan, as Weeping Snakes calls it. How well do you know it, Beaver?"

"I been there lots. It ain't gold-mining country, if that's what you're driving at. I don't even know what on earth, or from under it, them fools who found fool's gold in the creek took for color. There ain't enough quartz in the whole valley to bust a window with. It's right nice meadowland, dead flat in places, with the grass growing green and stirrup-high where it ain't overgrowed with trees. The banks of the creek are pipe clay, not rocky, and the bottom's mostly mud. So *you* tell *me* what them pilgrims panned and filed a mineral claim on. I'll be switched if I know!"

"They actually went to all the trouble of filing a claim?"

"Yep. Only the BIA tolt 'em they couldn't, even if the creek was filt to the brim with silver and gold. They started to sue the government over it, saying there was no call to set aside Indian lands with no Indians living on 'em half the time. Then they must have got bad news from the assay office, for they dropped the whole thing and rid off to hunt fool's gold somewheres else."

Longarm ran everything he knew about mineral claims through his head as they rode on. He knew more than most about the subject since, aside from having worked in some mines when he'd first come west after the War and hadn't learned to rope good yet, he'd sat in on many a court case involving the subject. Gents were always killing one another over claim jumping. He shook his head at last and said, "Clay and gravel pits don't work that far from civilization."

Beaver asked what he was talking about.

Longarm said, "Anything dug out of the ground is a mineral, so the mining laws allow one to stake a claim on the same. A rock quarry, a gravel pit, or a clay pit is legally no different than a gold mine, as far as the paperwork goes. But to make any profit at all on a valley paved with clay, you'd need to be close, mighty close, to a *market* for all your tedious digging. The nearest place I know where a clay mine could sell its offerings would be clean down in Denver. There's a couple of outfits down along the Platte making drain tiles, flower pots, and such, but they use the clay they dig almost out from under Denver to do so. There's a swamping big clay quarry just west of town. So no clay-digging operation this far north could possibly compete with it, sending little more than fancy dirt by rail. You say the stuff is *pipe* clay, Beaver?"

The old scout shrugged. "That's what she looks like. I hardly ever make pipes. It's a sort of dirty white clay, with soil and, come to think of it, *mica* mixed in. I recalls a morn when I was fishing in the creek down there. Didn't catch shit. The water was too muddy. But as I started across to the other bank with the sun ahint me, there was little winking stars of mica staring back at me."

Longarm smiled thinly and said, "That could account for its Indian name, as a starry land, and mica does fool a lot of ignorant prospectors."

"I knows what Kitlaztlan means in Ho. What was that about pipe clay, Longarm?"

"Well, the pure white clay they use to make pipes for Irishmen and dishes for other folk is rarer and more valuable than plain old country clay. But it's still a mighty long way to market, and even pipe clay can't be worth *that* much! I sure wish there was something down that way more worth a fight than water, timber, grass, and mud, though. I've been gnawing on a funny bone in my head ever since I talked to Weeping Snakes, but I just can't sink my thinking teeth into a flim-flam operation

126

with no profit motive I can see."

As they spoke they came to yet another creek across the trail. Longarm fell silent as he watched Beaver ford it, then heeled Blaze across after him. The creek wasn't deep, which was just as well, for halfway across Blaze put a hoof on a mossy rock that twisted out from under her and the two of them went down in the white water with a mighty splash.

Longarm went under for a moment and came up cursing in the waist-deep water just in time to see his hat rafting off downstream. First things coming first, he had to grope back to his confused mount and grab the wet, slippery reins to steady her and haul her on across. As they struggled up the far bank, he didn't see Beaver anywhere. He remounted and thought about that as he drew his .44 and made sure the barrel wasn't clogged. Then Beaver came back to the trail through the trees, waving Longarm's wet hat as he called out with a laugh, "Don't shoot. I'm on *your* side!"

Longarm chuckled and took his Stetson back. "You think sudden and you ride the same way, Beaver. Much obliged."

The scout shrugged modestly. "I had help. There's a beaver dam just around the bend. I must say you look cool and comfortable right now. But your methods of cooling off are a mite drastical for an old man with the rheumatiz."

Longarm said not to knock it until he tried it, and they rode on. For the first time Longarm, since he was in a hurry, took the lead. He was glad old Beaver hadn't taken advantage of such a golden opportunity to gun him just now. But, damn it, there went *another* infernal suspect!

# Chapter 11

They never caught up with Weeping Snakes on the trail that afternoon. As he and Beaver rode along the main drag of Freightown, Longarm was glad, and suspected he knew the reason. The tent show was set up in a mountain meadow on the far side of town, and no Indian with a lick of sense would have wanted to ride through directly. The dirty looks the two *whites* riding in as strangers got were enough to curdle milk in the cow. Freightown and its citizenry looked run down, depressed, and covered with soot from the switch engines chuffing back and forth in the marshaling yards all day and night. The recent rise in beef prices hadn't done much for the shanty-dwelling railroaders and their shanty-dwelling dependents. Since railroad building had died with a whimper during the financial panic of the Seventies, a lot of folk had been stranded out here, out of work, ever since. Longarm wondered how half of them ate. The railroads had started laying off as early as 1874.

Longarm and Beaver had managed to work up a thirst riding all that way under the now lower but still cruel sun. So they reined in at a saloon Beaver said hardly ever poisoned its customers to wet their whistles. The saloon was narrow and dark and smelled more like a coal cellar than a place to buy a beer. But the beer, when they got it, wasn't bad.

Old Beaver said he had to take a leak as well, so Longarm was alone at the bar when a skinny, wistful-looking old gal in a shimmy shirt that needed soap and water sidled up to him to ask if he'd like to go up to the cribs with her for two bits.

He shook his head politely and replied, "I just fell in a creek, and while most of me's dry again, I'll never get my boots back on if I don't let 'em dry all the way on my feet, ma'am."

"Pooh, you think I'm ugly. I may *be* ugly, but I can still screw better than any other whore in town, damn it!"

"I don't intend to dispute you, since I see no other fancy gals about who could possibly rival your charms. Business sure must be slow if a pretty little thing like you is offering her services for two bits. Ain't the going price three ways for two dollars, or seventy-five cents for a quick trick?"

She shrugged and said, "You'd be surprised how few men in this infernal town have two bits to buy *food* with. A gal has to adjust her price scale to what the market will bear, see?"

"It's been nice talking to you, but, no offense, I just ain't in the market for slap and tickle at any price," he told her.

She cussed him and moved on to pester someone else. Longarm had about finished his beer and wanted to get out of such dismal surroundings. So he looked around for old Beaver and spied him talking to another gent down at the far end of the bar. Longarm drained his schooner and moved down to join them, or try to. But the fatter and younger cuss jawing with Beaver saw him coming and headed for the outhouse out back as if he'd just noticed he was fixing to wet his fool self.

Longarm bellied up next to Beaver and said, "Well, at least I've seen a crook I *know* of in these parts."

Beaver blinked and asked, "Was he a crook? He just tolt me he was a cattle buyer. Didn't say his name. You know him, Longarm?"

"Know who he is, and he must have knowed I'd know it, from the way he lit out just now. They calls him Salty Sam Simmons down in Leadville. He's a con man who'll give you a real bargain on shares in nonexistent mines, or cut you in on a mine he aims to find if only you'll grubstake him to a few thousand. I wonder why he acted so scared just now. I ain't got enough on him to arrest him, more's the pity. What was he trying to sell you just now, Beaver?"

"Nothing. He said he was looking to buy beef. I tolt him I wasn't a cowboy, and the conversation was going downhill from there when you horned in."

"Did you tell him who you were or, more important, who you was riding with, and to where?"

"I didn't get a chance to tell him much more'n my handle. You sure ask dumb questions for a gent who *saw* the way he run when he discovered you were within a country mile of him!"

Longarm smiled sheepishly and said, "I must have hit my head on a rock in that creek. Let's get on out to the fairgrounds. I'll be interested to see if Salty Sam is out there waiting for us. The oily rascal has *something* guilty on his conscience, if I'm any judge of the breed at all."

They went back out, mounted back up, and rode on. They could hear the tent show before they could spot it ahead through the aspens sprouted like weeds along a strip of ground someone had cleared during the railroad boom and then forgot. A steam organ was wailing fit to bust in hopes of drawing folk from town. Whoever was playing it was so bad that Longarm failed to recognize the tune, if that was a tune and not a device in dire need of repairs.

The tent show was set up so a wide fairway of meadow grass ran between two rows of canvas booths, with the sleeping tents, wagons, and such back out of the way, closer to the water of another bitty creek. The grass of the fairway wasn't trampled much. There were more people working for the tent show at the moment than attending it. But the gate would likely grow some after sundown. Men with real jobs in town were expected to work until six on weekdays.

They tethered their ponies off to one side where they could graze some as well and strode on in, looking for Indians or other action. They didn't see much of either. Longarm decided to take advantage of the early evening lull to get the layout fixed firmly in his head, just in case. Beaver wandered off to see if any of the stands sold anything stronger than pink lemonade.

By the time Longarm had strolled to the end of the short fairway and back, he'd decided he'd seen many a two-bit tent show in his time, and that this one wasn't worth *that* much. They didn't have any freak shows or even any dirty ones. Save for a few booths peddling food and drink, the so-called whiskey served from an open barrel and so full of burnt sugar flies had drowned in it, most of the booths were devoted to pure games of chance, meaning not much chance at all. As he stood near a bottle toss pitch to light a cheroot the gal behind the counter called out, "How about it, cowboy? You look strong. All you have to do is knock the bottles down to win a genuine Venus de Milo your gal will just love!"

Longarm grinned at her and said, "If them ancient statues on your side shelf was covered with one more layer of dust they'd have to be dug up again, sis. To save you needless wear and tear on your lungs, I'm law and I know about the spikes that come up under them metal milk bottles to keep 'em from falling over more than you find profitable."

She looked uneasy. "I just work here, Sheriff. Talk to Mr. Duncan if you want a fix."

"I mean to," he told her. "Meanwhile, I'd like you to tell me about the two gals missing from this social improvement. Did you know either of 'em?"

She nodded. "Knew *both* of 'em. Not as well as they knew one another, of course. Edith and Joy was thick as thieves, which they was, in a way. You think *this* pitch is a gaff, wait till you bet against a pitch old *Joy* is running! They joined us down in Cheyenne. So I can't say for sure Edith *always* dealt blackjack crooked. An old Indian was whipping her pretty good until Mr. Duncan closed down the pitch for the night as busted. I was about here . . . I mean I was at this end of the fairway when all hell busted loose down near Fort Missoula, so I can't tell you just what happened while the Hey Rube was going on. I just grabbed the till and ducked out the back way when a bowie knife came whizzing past me. You're only supposed to throw *balls* at my bottles, and nothing at all at my *head*, see?"

He told her her head was too pretty to throw bowie knives at, and asked if anyone traveling with the show was likely to have pictures of the two missing gals. She shook her head and said, "Hell, no, why should they? Like I told you, Edith and Joy had just joined us a few stops down the line. They wasn't tied up with any of the gents with us, if that's what you mean."

He said that had been exactly what he meant and moved on to scout up the manager, Duncan.

Longarm didn't have far to look. Behind him the pitch gal shrilled a long coded whistle and a morose-looking gent dressed like a rich undertaker came out from between two booths to stare thoughtfully at Longarm. "I'm the owner, Sheriff. What's your beef? I thought the county and me had an agreement already signed and sealed."

Longarm chuckled. "I forgot to tell your bottle-pitch gal I'm federal. I'm reaching for my I.D., so leave that S&W on your hip alone, hear?"

Duncan didn't try to draw on him. He read the name off Longarm's I.D. and said, "I've heard of you. This calls for a celebration. We hardly ever entertain such well-known personages, Longarm."

He led the tall deputy over to the whiskey booth and told the gent serving burnt sugar and shellac thinner to get out the good stuff. The pitchman grinned, brought a bottle up from under the counter, and poured himself a shot glass of bourbon while he was at it. The three of them had a good belt and Duncan said to fill them up again before he asked Longarm what they could do for him.

Longarm repeated his questions regarding the missing girls. The tent-show boss told much the same tale as the bottle-pitch gal had and added, "They might have just gone on home, you know. Ohio, I think they said they came from. The usual story one hears when gals run off from a small, stuffy town together. Joy was the one who usually took the lead. Sassy little dishwater blonde with teasing eyes and rosebud lips that could outcuss a mule skinner. Edith was more sedate, but that ain't saying much. They was both sort of wild."

"You don't seem too worried about 'em."

"I ain't. Why should I be? I never got to kiss either one and, to tell the truth, I'd have had to fire them had they not vanished into thin air for whatever reason."

"Do tell? What was they doing that upset you so?"

Duncan grimaced and said, "Losing. I had Edith dealing blackjack and Joy on the wheel of fortune. Somehow I don't think they grasped the simple fact that this show is supposed to be a money-making proposition, not a charitable organization."

Longarm nodded understandingly. "I noticed how dusty the prizes seem to be in the bottle pitch. I take it the two gals were the ones old Weeping Snakes won so much off before the trouble started?"

Duncan frowned and said, "As a matter of fact, I'd taken them both out from behind their counters by then. That's why nobody can say for sure where they was when the Hey Rube went up. I don't know how that old medicine man does it, but he was whipping hell out of the relief I sent in when some cowhands took umbrage and all hell broke loose."

Longarm cocked an eyebrow and took another sip of bourbon. "No offense, Duncan, but don't we both know it's just pure impossible for even a white man to beat the house consistent?"

"That's what I just said. The cowhands thought the old buck was cheating, too. It must have riled them some to see a redskin winning hard cash when they couldn't even take home a stuffed toy."

Longarm sighed and said, "A thing like that might

even piss *me* off, and I'm sweet-natured. But let's see if I got the house odds straight. Most of your pitches pay off in merchandise, like door stoppers made to look like cats, for some fool reason, or Venus de Milo dolls made of genuine plaster that anyone would be proud to have about the cabin?"

Duncan nodded. "Sure. A man in my line has to have *some* control of his cash flow, and most of these hicks don't have enough to play for high stakes anyways. So the few games of chance that pay off in cash are down at this end where I can keep an eye on 'em."

Longarm followed Duncan's gaze and saw that, sure enough, a wheel of fortune booth and a blackjack layout were set up next to one another just down the line. Neither one was doing any business at the moment. The gent in the wheel of fortune booth was reading a newspaper. "I see you replaced the two missing gals with present-and-accounted-for gents," Longarm said.

Duncan nodded. "New to the show, but not unknown in the profession. They were the ones on duty, as you see them, the night the two sassy gals vanished into the noisy dark. Want to talk to them about it?"

Longarm shook his head. "Not hardly. If the gals had jumped over their counters at 'em they'd have likely noticed. If they knew how Weeping Snakes was winning, they'd have likely told you about it by now, right?"

Duncan smiled wryly and said, "That's for damned sure. I asked them. The old Bannock has to be a professional magician, for his skills go beyond the mechanics of professional gambling. They tell the same tale as the missing gals. The old buck just stood there with his hands inside that red blanket he wears, when he wasn't actually placing a bet or raking in his winnings, without tipping or even saying thanks. Nobody spotted any suspicious moves on the part of the braves with him, either. That old Indian is just plain *spooky!*"

Longarm got out a cheroot and lit up, taking his time about it, before he said, "I don't believe in spooks. So I got to ask you a serious question, and I want you to mull it over some before you answer it. You know I'm federal, and that I ain't allowed to enforce gambling laws even when I want to."

"So?"

"So I want you to tell me, man to man, just what mechanical devices old Weeping Snakes has to get around to win so consistent."

Duncan refused to meet Longarm's eyes. "Hell, the odds favor the house, even betting upright and true. You see, there's only one chance in twenty-four that the number you pick on the wheel of fortune will come to a stop, even spinning freely, while the odds are always with the dealer in blackjack and, naturally, the customer never gets to deal, so—"

"So stop bullshitting me and get down to the real part," Longarm cut in. "You wouldn't have relieved them gals had you thought they was dealing honest agin a run of luck. You thought they might be in cahoots with the Indian for a kickback. But when you put more loyal and trustworthy servants on the job, Weeping Snakes still kept winning. So you had somebody start a fight to save your show from getting cleaned out. True or false?"

Duncan sighed sheepishly and said, "All but the last part. The cowhands who started up with the Indians weren't working for me."

"But the old medicine man was beating a wheel of fortune with a brake and a blackjack layout with a stacked deck, right?"

"Damn it, I *said* it was spooky."

"Spooky, hell! It was pure *impossible!* If Weeping Snakes wasn't cheating, someone had to be cheating *for* him. That's a plain law of nature, Duncan."

The tent-show boss shrugged. "All right, I'd best just confess all to you, then. I've ordered my help to let the old buck win because I admire noble savages and this business of mine is just a hobby, see?"

Longarm nodded wearily and said, "When you're right, you're right. It don't make sense no matter how you slice it." Then he spotted motion down at the far end of the fairway and added, "Well, here we go again."

Duncan followed his gaze and muttered, "Oh, shit!" For Weeping Snakes was coming their way on foot, backed by a dozen of his braves. Irene Woodford was with them, but not to back Weeping Snakes, from the way she was jawing at him as they came down the fairway side by side. As they got within earshot Longarm heard her pleading, "You can't risk your money like this, damn it! You're just going to wind up flat broke, and I've told you and told you I can't get any rations or allotments for you and your band if you won't agree to accept me as your agent!"

"You can be our agent, Saltu daughter, as long as you don't try to tell us what to *do!*" the old medicine chief said. "Heya, there stands Longarm. My heart soars to see him. He has good teotl, too. Maybe we can bet together and take all the money they have here tonight."

Longarm glanced at the red sky to the west and saw that it was almost nightfall. But nothing else the old man was saying made much sense. As they joined him and Duncan at the whiskey booth, the counterman hastily got the bottle out of sight.

Irene turned to Longarm. "I've been arguing with him all the way along the dusty trail, and I could have gotten

137

as much agreement out of any number of trees we passed! Maybe *you* can make him listen, Custis."

Longarm shrugged and said, "Hear me, Weeping Snakes. You can't beat the house. I have spoken."

The old Bannock grinned like a mean little kid. "We shall see. I need more money to buy a homeland for my people. I came here to win more money. If I don't get to bet tonight nobody gets to bet tonight. *I* have spoken, too!"

Longarm turned to Duncan. "There's no law saying you have to keep every booth open. I don't reckon he's out to take all your stuffed toys or door stops."

Duncan hesitated, stared down the fairway towards town, and said, "You'd be surprised how little profit there is in door stops. I *can't* shut down the gambling booths that pay cash, damn it. Not if I expect anyone to stay here long enough to matter."

Longarm saw a clump of railroaders coming, too. "Well, it's your tent show, old son," he said. "I got to find out what happened to old Beaver. You want to help me look for him, Miss Woodford?"

The girl from the BIA let him lead her off to the side, but asked why on earth the old scout couldn't take care of himself. Longarm said, "He likely can and, if he can't, I ain't his mother. I just wanted to jaw with you alone. Not courting. Serious."

"Oh, you think if we put our heads together we can keep Weeping Snakes from losing back all the money he's won?"

"I ain't Weeping Snakes's mother, neither. I ain't worried about him going broke. For one thing, you'd likely find him and his band easier to manage if they was more dependent on you for bread and beans next winter."

"Then what *are* we talking about, Custis?"

"Trouble. This town is tougher than Fort Missoula

138

and we know what happened there when local toughs got to pushing and shoving. I got enough on my plate out here without I got to worry about yet another she-male vanishing in the confusion."

"I can take care of myself, thank you very much."

He shook his head. "No offense, ma'am, but I doubt you could possibly be as tough as two carnival gals put together. And even if you are, I like to work alone in a firefight. So I don't want you about when and if another one starts. The evening's still young. So we likely have time to carry you and your pony into town where you'll be safe. We'll put your mount in the livery and you in a hotel I noticed near the depot."

"You'll do no such thing!" she protested. "I didn't follow my Indian wards all this way to leave them undefended!"

He chuckled and said, "They won't be undefended. I'll be here to watch the old man's back if the dozen braves he brought with him all fall down in a heap at once. The point is that I can't watch everybody's back at the same time. So I'm fixing to stow your sweet behind safely out of the way. When it's over, I'll come back and get you. Then I'll be proud to ride you back to Fort Missoula, see?"

She told him in as ladylike a tone as she could manage to go to hell. But by now he'd managed to get her to a shadowy stretch of the fairway in the tricky sunset light. So he sighed as if beaten and offered his hand as if to shake on it. Irene automatically put her own hand out, and before she could even wonder why, he'd snapped handcuffs on her wrists and said, "All right, you're under arrest, then. Let's go. Don't make a fuss. It could harm a lady's rep if anyone saw her getting hauled off to jail kicking and screaming."

"Are you crazy?" she protested, firmly but sedately

resisting as he herded her between two booths and along the back way to where they could round up their mounts. She gave up trying to pull her right wrist free, but told him he had no infernal right to arrest a fellow federal agent who hadn't done anything wrong. He shook his head and told her, "You was wrong to ride into such dangerous surroundings without a gun to call your own, ma'am. It's agin the law to obstruct a federal officer on duty, and having to worry about you as well as me out here could obstruct hell out of me. So you got two choices, ma'am. You can let me check you into a hotel that might or might not have bedbugs, or you can spend the night in a jail that'll have 'em for sure as a . . . well, a federal witness will likely satisfy the local law. They has to put *something* down when they book you, see?"

"Oh, no, you can't make me spend the night in *jail!*"

"Sure I can. I put folk in jail all the time. I'm good at it. But if *you* want to be good, the hotel by the depot will do just as well."

She hesitated, then tried to keep the cunning out of her voice as she replied, "All right, I'll go to the hotel with you as the lesser of two evils."

He knew what she planned to do once he left her there. But he was cunning, too, so he decided not to mention before they got there that he intended to cuff her to the bedpost.

# Chapter 12

By the time Longarm got back to the tent show it was dark everywhere but on the well-lit fairway. A fair-sized crowd was working at losing its money under the harsh glare of the fancy lighting. The tent-show operator couldn't have used the new Edison bulbs even if he had wanted to. But since old Edison had scared hell out of the coal-oil lantern industry a couple of years back, they'd met his competition head on with bigger and better mantles that cast as good a light or better than the newfangled electrical notions.

Weeping Snakes was easy to spot with the lamplight bouncing off his bright red blanket. As Longarm approached he saw the old scout, Beaver, in earnest conversation with the Bannock leader on the far side. As Longarm got within earshot, Beaver was pleading, "Don't *do* it, damn it! It's a con game! You ain't got a chance!"

Longarm saw what Beaver meant when he got close

141

enough to see into the booth the Indian was standing in front of. Longarm sighed as he saw it was the old shell game. A not-bad-looking gal who should have been ashamed of herself was moving three gold-painted walnut shells about on the slick oilcloth surface of her counter as she pitched, "First you see it and then you don't, Chief. Guess which shell the pea is under and win double your money!"

Weeping Snakes brought a skinny brown hand out from under the blanket to point at a shell, saying, "That one, pretty lady."

The carnival gal turned over the shell to expose the "pea," which was usually sponge rubber that squished easily into the folds of even a pinky. "By golly, you guessed right!" she said. "It's a good thing for me you wasn't betting that time, Chief."

Weeping Snakes placed a twenty-dollar gold piece on the oilcloth. "I bet now. I win forty dollars if I guess right again?"

The girl stared soberly down at the considerable bet. Then she started moving the shells about as she somehow managed to keep from grinning like a fox in a henhouse. Longarm could see from where he was standing which shell the pea was supposed to be under despite all the shuffling about. That was what made the shell game such a trap for suckers. He knew by now that the so-called pea was out from under the shells entirely and that it hardly mattered which one the fool Indian picked. But Weeping Snakes picked the same one Longarm would have, had he been a fool, and the girl turned it over with a grin.

Then her grin got sort of sickly.

The pea was there.

Weeping Snakes said, "Good. You owe me forty dollars, pretty lady."

The girl stared down at the pea as if it had just popped out from under a rock at her with it's stinger raised to strike. She gulped and said, "I sure do. Would you like to let the money ride, Chief?"

Weeping Snakes nodded. Beaver and Longarm said at the same time, "Don't!" For anyone could see now how she was setting him up for a real plucking. But Weeping Snakes said, "I got twenty. I won forty. I bet all sixty, pretty lady."

She took him up on it, of course, and by now the heavier than usual action had attracted others to watch as the gal skated her shells all over the counter, then stopped, stepped back, and told Weeping Snakes to find the pea again.

He did. A collective gasp welled up from the crowd and the gal looked as if she was about to puke. "You sure are lucky, Chief," she said.

Weeping Snakes said, "Yes, the spirits told me I would be. You owe me one hundred and twenty dollars, pretty lady."

She gulped. "Oh, I forgot to tell you. The house limit is a hundred dollars, Chief. I fear you just broke my bank."

Weeping Snakes turned to Longarm to ask, "Do you know what she is talking about, old enemy?"

Longarm nodded at him but told the girl, "It won't wash, honey. You knew what the bet was when you took it in front of God and all the rest of us. Give the man his money. For I am federal law, and it's a federal offense to cheat Indians."

The other whites in the crowd laughed as the red-faced shell-game gal paid out a hundred and twenty in cash but told Weeping Snakes she didn't want to play with him any more. As Longarm led him away he saw other suckers moving in to take the Bannock's place at the counter, so he knew she'd survive in the end. He told the medicine man, politely but flatly, "All right. I don't know how you're doing it, but it's got to stop. You can't just go about cheating white folk so brazen, Weeping Snakes. They're sure to get mad at you again."

Weeping Snakes looked innocent. "I don't know what you mean. I told you my medicine was strong. But did you see me touch those shells the pretty lady moved herself?"

"I did not. But said pretty lady was palming them rubber peas on you, and you wasn't supposed to win, damn it!"

Weeping Snakes shrugged. "I think I try the wheel of fortune now. It has a four on it and four is a spirit number."

On his far side, Beaver said, "Longarm, this can't go on much longer. I'll cover your back if you'll cover mine and we'll both try to save this fool Indian, agreed?"

Longarm said that made sense, but tried to tell Weeping Snakes to ease up as they all approached the wheel of fortune with the old man's silent braves behind them. He'd thought Irene was stubborn when he'd cuffed her, cussing, to the bedpost at the hotel. But Weeping Snakes didn't even answer as he stepped up to the wheel of fortune booth and called out, "Heya, fat man in funny suit, I got a hundred dollars to bet wheel stops at four next time."

The pudgy pitchman behind the counter cast a thoughtful eye on the money the Bannock was spreading on the counter between them. "You'd best let me check with the boss first, Chief, for you are talking about a thousand dollars if you win," he said.

"I know," Weeping Snakes said. "I need much money to buy valley of Kitlaztlan."

The pitchman whistled. The soberly dressed Duncan

materialized from the crowd and stared morosely at Weeping Snakes. "I just came from the shell-game pitch," he said. "We don't cater to professional card sharks here. This tent show is only meant to be family entertainment."

"Hear me. This is not a card game," the Indian said. "It is a wheel of fortune. I am standing here. The wheel is there. You are woman-hearted if you are afraid to let me play."

The mutterings from the other whites crowding around to see the fun were somewhat ominous, but divided. Some seemed annoyed at an Indian being there in the first place, while others thought Duncan was letting his own race down by refusing to skin the savage fair and square. The tent-show boss grimaced, shrugged, and said, "All right. One spin. That's it, win or lose. Agreed?"

"Sure," Weeping Snakes said, "I *always* win."

Duncan nodded at his pitchman. But by the time the wheel was spinning Longarm had quietly slipped around to the back of the canvas booth, his .44 drawn casually. He could see the grass ahead by the lamplight coming through the thin canvas. There was nobody back here pulling strings or doing anything else. He heard a roar from out on the fairway and as he moved back, puzzled, he heard someone shouting, "The old buck's done her again! The fool wheel stopped on four like a gunshot clock!"

Longarm rejoined the group around the front of the booth as Weeping Snakes was putting a thousand dollars away under his blanket. Duncan was saying, "That's it, Chief. I don't know how you're doing it and I'd be a fool to accuse a man backed by a tribe of Indians of cheating even if I *knew* the gaff! But from now on your house limit is five hundred a night, and tonight you've passed it."

Weeping Snakes asked Longarm, "Can he do that?"

Longarm nodded and explained, "He just did. It's considered fair to set a house limit as long as you sets it ahead of time. Five hundred is generous for a tent show, considering you ain't really supposed to win at *all*."

Weeping Snakes shrugged. "You Saltu are all sissies. I go now, but I come back tomorrow night for my five hundred dollars. We make camp up in hills above town. I don't have enough money to buy my land yet."

Duncan shook his head. "You can camp on the city dump for all I care. But we won't be here tomorrow night. This gate ain't worth two nights in Freighttown. So we're moving up to Superior in hopes somebody in Montana has some money to lose for a change!"

Longarm ran a mental finger over his mental map of Montana Territory. "That's quite a haul for one day, ain't it?" he asked.

Duncan shrugged and said, "All right, we'll take two days. Got to set up in more profitable surroundings before we're flat busted."

Weeping Snakes frowned. "Hear me, I know where Superior is. You go. Take wheel of fortune with you. I meet you in Superior and you have five hundred ready. I have spoken."

As he turned on his heel and marched off down the fairway with his braves trailing, Duncan sighed. "I wish he hadn't said that. How long do you figure that fool Indian will trail us, Longarm?"

Longarm replied, "Can't rightly say. He's enjoying the game he's playing with you. Indians always start talking like that when they're having fun with us. He don't act so heap chief in frontum cigar store when he's his ownself."

Beaver spat and said, "Anyone can see he's playing

cat-and-mouse games, Longarm. But how in the hell is he *doing* it?"

Longarm turned to the plumper man behind the counter to ask soberly, "What happened to your brake, friend?"

The pitchman shot a nervous glance at his boss. When Duncan nodded, he shook his head with a puzzled frown. "I don't know. The wheel was supposed to stop at seven."

Duncan told him to try it again. He moved back and gave it a whirl, and it stopped at seven. Duncan said flatly, "He suckered us back. We have to figure out *how,* God damn it!" Then he turned to Longarm almost to plead, "Isn't there some limit to how far an Indian is allowed to stray from his reservation, damn it?"

"The Bannock ain't agreed to where their reserve *is* at the moment," Longarm said. "So that makes enforcing such regulations tough. Mind if I make a suggestion?"

Duncan nodded and Longarm said, "Try running the games pure honest the next time."

"Are you serious? Have you any idea what an overhead I have to cover, Longarm?"

"I know it sounds bad. But I was out back just now when he skinned you, and there wasn't anyone working the wheel behind the canvas for him. It might be interesting to see what happened if you just let the wheel spin free. I know nobody but the pitchman is supposed to even know where the brake pedal is, but unless we buy his heap big medicine, *someone* braked that wheel on four for him just now!"

Duncan said he would consider such a drastic course of action and they shook on it. As Longarm turned away, Beaver asked him where he was going.

"Show's over here for now," Longarm said. "Got to see a lady about some other matters, if she's still talking to me."

Beaver said in that case he'd see him later, if at all,

adding he knew some ladies in Freightown himself. So they split up grinning.

Longarm had left Blaze in the livery near the hotel with Irene's mount. But it wasn't far to walk, as he'd discovered coming the other way. The main street was on the far side of the railyards and when he got that far he had to stop as a train of casual freight rolled in slow behind a 2-6-4 Baldwin. He had plenty of time, so he leaned against a telegraph pole as he waited for them to get the train out of his way.

The last cars and the caboose rolled by and Longarm started on across the tracks. Then he saw a familiar figure drop off the platform of the caboose, shouting, "Take her on into the siding, Mike. I got a gal to look up whilst we're stuck here for a spell."

Longarm managed to get pretty close to the Emperor Edwards before the brakeman spotted him, gasped, and started running.

It didn't work. Hardly anybody ran faster than Longarm, even in boots over rails and ties. As the Emperor glanced back and saw how Longarm was gaining on him, he tried ducking down the line between two lines of empty boxcars. It was sort of dark as they ran along the track with boxcars looming on either side. But Longarm was too close now for the bully to lose that way. He tried a sideways leap through a gap in the cars. As Longarm tore through after him he heard a strangled gasp of pain. The next time he saw the Emperor the rascal was down on the ties, tugging at one shin with both hands. Longarm slowed to an ominous walk as he moved in to say pleasantly, "I've been hoping we'd meet again, you son of a bitch. How come you're sitting down like that?"

"Don't stomp me, Longarm!" Edwards whined. "It ain't *fair,* damn it."

Longarm said, "Hell, I know that. Stand up so's I can knock you down again."

"I can't! I'm stuck! My ankle's caught in a damned switch and I can't get it loose!"

Longarm moved closer, hunkered down in the dim light, and struck a match. "You're right. Your big old foot popped through between the close-set rails, and damned if they ain't bear-trapped on your skinnier ankle."

"Tell me something I don't already know, damn it! Help me get loose afore a train comes through on this line! I'll fight you if that's what you want. But you got to get me out of this fix!"

Longarm took out two cheroots and handed one down to the Emperor. "I might. I might not even whip your ass, if you'll just tell me some things I don't know."

"Damn it, Longarm, they'll be switching all over these yards as they recombine that freight I just come in on, and if the switch engine comes this way *backwards...*"

"Yeah, if it's backing a couple of cars as well, there's not a chance in hell they'll spot you in time. Like I was saying, I'd sure like to know who told you to seal that young bo and me up and send us out to a deserted siding down by Kate's Crossing."

"Oh, hell, Longarm, can't you take a joke? I knew you'd get out sooner or later. Just wanted to throw a little scare in you, that's all."

Longarm struck another match to light both their smokes. But the trapped brakeman didn't have his stuck in his now-pale ugly face. Longarm shrugged, lit his own, and said, "Before you get run over by a train, I'd best save time by telling you I know for a fact you are full of pure shit, Emperor. You know as well as me that a gutless wonder like you never would have played joke

149

one on a man of my rep, had someone not told you I'd never get out alive to come looking for you. You couldn't have known, ahead, that I was boarding that freight out of Denver. So somebody met you somewhere along the line and made it worth your while to do what you did. You can tell me who it was, or you can just sit here and hope someone else comes along to free you in time. I ain't got time to argue with you about it. We're keeping a lady waiting. So what's it going to be?"

Emperor Edwards whimpered, "I don't know his name. He was waiting on the freight platform at Fort Missoula. He asked if it was true you was aboard. When I said it was he gave me a hundred dollars to do what I done. That's all I know."

Longarm curled his lip and said, "You know more than that. For one thing, he promised you I'd never get out of that boxcar alive, didn't he?"

"Not in so many words. I swear. He just said I wouldn't have to worry about you ever coming after me to pay me back!"

"Well, now you can see how wrong he was. So what did he look like? Everybody has to look like *somebody,* damn it!"

The Emperor tugged desperately at his shin as he pleaded, "Please, Longarm, I don't want to die *that* way, neither! He swore he'd come after me himself if I ever talked, and he looked like a gunslick!"

"He likely was. I'm still waiting for a better description."

Longarm might have gotten one, but just then a rifle flashed from the pitch-black gap between the parked cars and Longarm threw himself away from the trapped brakeman to land on his side, rolling like hell as he drew his own gun. He was out of line with the gap now, so to draw another bead on him the rifleman would have to come out in the open.

He didn't, so Longarm tried it another way. He crabbed sideways on his belly between the wheels of the nearest boxcar to get into the same dark lane the bastard had fired from.

It didn't work. The bastard was long gone, though he'd left his stink behind him. Longarm got up and walked through the same gunsmoke-scented gap to see how the Emperor had made out. The brakeman didn't have to worry about getting run over by a train now. The high-powered rifle had blown the far side of his head across the cinders to the south. Longarm heard shouts and running feet on more of the same cinders. He holstered his gun and moved out quietly. He had enough to worry about without explaining every mess he left in his wake to gents who couldn't do anything helpful about them.

# Chapter 13

When Longarm let himself into the hotel room where he had left Irene alone to stew in safety, he found that she had cried herself to sleep, fully dressed on the bed with her wrist hitched to the brass above her head. He bent over her to unlock the cuff. Her eyes popped open and she flinched in fear. He smiled down at her and said, "War's over. Weeping Snakes managed to win more modest this evening, and by now him and his braves are camped in the hills somewhere. Sure hope it's on federal range."

As he freed her, she sat up and ran her hands over her riding skirts as if to make sure they were still in place. "Oh, I must have fainted, you brute," she said. "I hope you didn't take advantage of me while I was unconscious."

He sat on the edge of the bed beside her as he replied in a disgusted tone, "Don't talk dumb. There's no way to get even a hand up them split skirts enough to matter and, if there was, you gals always *know* when you've been taken advantage of."

She blushed beet-red. He hadn't expected a sensible gal her age to be a *total* virgin. As if to change the subject, she asked him to tell her about the goings-on out at the tent show, so he did. She couldn't figure out how Weeping Snakes was doing it, either, although, being such a sensible gal, she agreed he had to be doing something sneaky to win so regularly. She asked, "Couldn't he have used sleight-of-hand on the girl with the shells?"

Longarm said, "He must have. But how? He never went anywheres *near* them shells, and *she* was the one doing the sleight-of-hand. The pea is sponge rubber. The con artist can crush it small as a grain of sand and hold it most anywhere *but* under any infernal shell."

"What if she was in on it with him, Custis?"

"That would work, of course, but only up to a point. The point of a flim-flam tent show is to make money, not to lose it on purpose."

"I've heard of a professional gambler working against his own house with a confederate, though."

"So have I. So has Duncan, most likely, and he packs a double-action .45 under his moody frock coat. One or even two carnival folk letting a confederate win that heavy might just skim inside impossible. But Weeping Snakes can't be in cahoots with the whole infernal outfit!"

She asked why not. It struck Longarm as a mighty stupid question, but he'd gotten more than one good tip from fools, so he always listened and sometimes even replied politely to a mighty dumb suggestion. He said, "Look, if for any reason at all Duncan wanted to make Weeping Snakes a rich Indian, he could simply *give* him the damned money. The old Indian's caused at least one out-and-out brawl and unsettled hell out of Duncan's business. Why go to all that trouble when we both know

153

Weeping Snakes would gladly accept a peace offering from any white man as his due?"

She said she had no idea, and asked what was going to happen next. "Well, there's more'n one way to skin the next cat down the pike," he told her. "I could take you back to Fort Missoula and put you to bed right, for openers."

"Sir! Whatever are you suggesting?"

"I meant in your own bed at the Indian agency office, damn it. Whether you invite me for a nightcap or not is up to you. On the other hand, it's late, I suspicion that at least one rascal with a rifle is gunning for me, and escorting a lady half the night along a dark mountain trail don't sound so smart. We got this room hired until high noon tomorrow, so why don't we just stay here for now?"

"Oh, dear, that *is* what you're suggesting!"

"Damn it, girl, I wish you she-males would let a gent make at least a move in your direction before you tell him the answer is no! I know you're pretty and you know I know you're pretty. But how do you know I want to even kiss you?"

"No girl needs to be told what a man has on his mind. You men are all alike!"

"You women are, too. Sometimes it make a poor boy feel sheer insulted to know all you gals have the same thing in mind as he passes by the beauty parlor, minding his own business."

She laughed, told him he was a big goof, and asked him what the rest of his cat-skinning might involve.

"Well, Fort Missoula is south, far enough, and the fool Bannock mean to follow the tent show a day's ride or more *north,* to Superior," he said. "By the time I rode you home, then retraced my steps, I could *miss* what happens next, and I ain't sure I'd better."

"Oh, I'd better ride to Superior with you in the morning, then. Weeping Snakes is still my ward, you know."

"*I* know it. *He* don't seem to. You can't ride north with me. But while we're on the subject of wayward Indians, just how far do the Bannock have to stray before the BIA considers 'em incorrigible?"

She said she didn't know. He said, "I might. When Dull Knife led the Cheyenne off their reserve and headed back to their old hunting grounds they only got a few days' ride before the government declared 'em Hostiles."

"But Weeping Snakes isn't *on* the warpath, Custis!"

"Neither was Dull Knife, till folk started shooting at him. He just wanted to go home. But Indians wandering all about make white folk nervous. If the Bannock follow that tent show much farther, you and me won't have much say in the matter. The territorial government will put pressure on Washington to do some damned something about the wandering Bannock, and I don't have to tell you this is an election year and that your BIA and my Justice Department as well as the War Department are run by politicians."

She nodded soberly. "You're right. We have to stop them and turn them around. But *how,* short of pointing guns at them?"

"I'll do all the gun pointing that might be needed. Might be a slicker way to skin that cat, too. Don't make much sense to gun an Indian to keep him from getting gunned. What say you take off your duds and turn in for some real sleep? We can jaw about it some more over breakfast in the morning."

She stared up owlishly at him and licked her lips. He said, "There you go, taking us men for granted again. I'm going downstairs now to hire another room. You just lock the door after me and do whatever you've a mind to."

He grumped down to the lobby, annoyed at her for being so sure he wanted her and even more annoyed with himself because she was right. At the desk he met Beaver, of all folk, jawing with the night clerk. He said, "Howdy, old son. You staying at this hotel, too?"

Beaver grinned. "Nope. *You* are, with that BIA gal, you rascal. I've been asking all over town for you, and I just now caught up with you at last."

"You sure have. What's up?"

"Weeping Snakes is camped upslope not more'n a mile outside of town. He paid a rancher cash to let him. I just come from there, after talking myself blue in the face at the ornery old redskin. He's bound and determined to ride on north after that tent show."

Longarm nodded and said, "He's as tedious as them German kids as followed the pied piper. Nobody could talk *them* out of it, neither. But I'll have to give it a try, as soon as I can think up something new to say."

Beaver asked, "Did you hear about the shooting over to the railyards not too long ago?"

It was a sin to lie to one's elders, so Longarm just asked who had shot whom. That was a question he really wanted to know the answer to. Beaver said, "Railroad brakeman got hit with a rifle ball fired by a person or persons unknown. Didn't get *his* name, neither. They was still fussing about it as I come across the tracks from Weeping Snakes's camp. Seems they couldn't pick him up to carry him off because his laig was caught in a switch. Ain't that a bitch?"

Longarm shrugged, turned to the clerk, and paid for the room right next door to the one he'd already hired. The clerk handed him the key but couldn't resist smirking. "What happened, the wife has a headache?" he asked.

"How would *you* like a headache to go with your big mouth?"

"Just funning, Deputy. Can't you take a joke?"

"Not lately. Had too many jokes played on me since I come to Montana."

He consulted his watch, nodded to himself, and told Beaver it was early enough to visit Indian medicine men before turning in. Beaver said he'd be proud to show him the way.

It only took them a few minutes to get mounted up at the nearby livery and ride out to the Bannock camp. Since Weeping Snakes and his escort of young men had left their women and kids near Kate's Crossing, they'd pitched no tipi ring and were mostly just stretched out on blanket-covered grass around their night fire. As Longarm and Beaver rode in, half of the Bannock were sitting up with thoughtful hands on their handy guns. So Longarm knew they'd posted night pickets too slick to be spotted by late-night visitors. Now, if only he could keep the *Bannock* from jumping *whites* at night . . .

Weeping Snakes came to greet them as they dismounted near the fire. He said, "We have eaten. But if you have hunger we can put more mush on the fire."

Longarm shook his head. "Didn't come to dine. Came to show you some card tricks, old son."

Even Beaver looked surprised as Longarm took out a poker deck and hunkered down by the fire to ask, "What do we want to play, gents, regular poker or three-card monte? Three-card monte goes a heap faster, and I ain't got all night."

The old Bannock hunkered down across from him, grinning in the firelight as he asked mildly, "What are we playing for, old enemy?"

Longarm took out all the cash he had on him and spread it in the dirt. "I'm betting money agin you. But I don't want your money. I want you to bet me *serious*, unless you ain't got the gizzard for *real* gambling!"

Weeping Snakes said, "Hear me. My teotl is strong. What do you hope to win off me, *blood?* If I win I take your money. If you win you can cut me any place you want. This will be fun!"

"I got no use for your blood, neither," Longarm said. "If I win, you take your band back down to Fool's Gold Valley and let Miss Woodford set up a proper agency for you. Deal?"

Weeping Snakes scowled. "Wait. I must think about this bet. I want to follow that tent show and take all their money away from them. How can I do that if we go back to Kitlaztlan?"

"You can't. That's the point of this here game. If you're afraid my medicine is stronger than yourn, don't play me. I can likely find some Saltu kids with more sand in their craw if you're afraid."

It worked. The old man scowled and said, "I know how the three-card game is played. It is like the shell game, only easier. Deal."

Longarm did, flicking the three cards back and forth in the flickering firelight as the old man watched intently. When Longarm said, "Go ahead," Weeping Snakes turned over a card with a triumphant grin. The grin faded when he saw he'd picked the wrong one.

He said, "Hear me, you cheated! Ometeotl told me in a vision that no Saltu had my powers!"

"I've had some great dreams, too. Wish *half* of 'em had come true. I just whipped you fair and square in front of your Great Spirit and all us smaller gents. But have it your way, you old sissy. Here's the three cards face up. Note I got nothing up my sleeves. Now I'm gonna turn them back over, and this time it's for keeps, unless you want me to think you're not a man of his word."

158

Weeping Snakes said, "My word is good, you Saltu bastard! Deal!"

Longarm did, and again Weeping Snakes failed to pick the high card. It would have surprised hell out of Longarm if he had, since he'd naturally palmed it and switched a deuce for it.

For a long time Weeping Snakes said nothing. "Look at it this way, old son," Beaver said, "you're still ahead the money you've won off that tent show, and Longarm may have saved you from losing it back now that your medicine's deserted you."

The old man frowned. "I don't understand this at all. I beat those *other* Saltu almost every time. It is true I lost the first time I played poker with cowhands in a saloon. But no doubt they were cheating, too."

Longarm swore softly. "All right. I'll deal again and you tell me *how* I'm cheating, you fool crybaby!"

But Weeping Snakes shook his head and said, "I bet you. You won. I will take my people back to Kitlaztlan as I promised. But will you tell me where you got your stronger teotl, old enemy?"

Longarm chuckled. "Her name was Trixie and she dealt three-card monte in Dodge when I first come west. Getting to know her was sort of complimentful, since she bet me a night in bed with her agin a month's pay and damned if I didn't win, with her dealing. I'll show you how it's done if you'll tell us how you skinned them tent-show rascals, pard. I'd surely like to know how you put peas back under shells after the dealer's palmed 'em."

Weeping Snakes said he didn't know what he meant and insisted he'd won fair and square at the tent show, allowing for his medicine, of course. So Longarm never told him how to cheat at three-card monte, which was likely just as well, when one studied on it.

# Chapter 14

Longarm and Beaver rode back to town together. At the livery, Beaver said he still had to find that certain lady and treat her right. As they stepped back outside to part friendly the scout said, "I'll likely see you again at Fort Missoula if either of us gets to sleep late after sunrise. You want me to make sure the Bannock do as they promised, or do *you* aim to, Longarm?"

The tall deputy said, "I don't reckon either of us needs to. The old man's a gent. He'll keep his word. You'd best get word to the army that he's coming back their way, peaceable."

Beaver shrugged. "I'll likely get back well ahead of 'em, even if she makes me flapjacks for breakfast. You know how pokey Indians move when they ain't going no place in a hurry. Weeping Snakes will likely take longer than usual getting home, now, as sore as he is about losing his medicine. How'd you lose him his medicine, Longarm? I was watching close, and I didn't see you switching cards."

"You wasn't supposed to. I'm looking forward to breakfast, too. So we'd best call it a night, and if we don't meet again it was nice meeting you, old son."

They shook on it and each went his own way. Back at the hotel, Longarm let himself into the room next to Irene's as quiet as a church mouse, or he tried to. Some fool had left a bentwood chair by the foot of the bed for him to knock over in the dark.

He struck a match and lit the bedside lamp. Then he put the chair back on its feet and used it to drape things over as he got undressed. He moved naked to the washstand in the corner to rub his hide down a mite for bed after the long, hot day and the sort of sweaty card game out at the Indian camp. When he heard a soft tap on the door he grabbed a towel with one hand and his .44 with the other before asking who it was.

It was Irene. She said she couldn't sleep and that she'd heard him coming in. She had more duds on than he did, though she'd shucked her riding skirts to wander about the hallway at all hours in her chemise. He shut the door behind her and locked the barrel bolt. She looked up at him uneasily and he explained, "I ain't locking you in. I'm locking some rascal with a rifle out."

"You . . . you don't have any clothes on, Custis!"

"Sure I do. This towel covers all my important parts, and *you* ain't one to talk. Did anyone ever tell you what grand legs you got, girl?"

She sat on the bed and crossed her bare thighs as if she thought that might do some good. "I can't stay long. I just came to see what you've been up to all this while," she told him.

Actually, if it got much more up she figured to *see* it

despite the towel around his middle, so Longarm sat down beside her, put his pistol on the night table under the lamp, and brought her up to date. When he got to the part about Weeping Snakes promising to go home and behave himself for now at least, Irene gasped, "Oh, you darling man! I could kiss you for saving my wards from their own foolishness!"

He reeled her in and kissed her good. Irene kissed back at first, but as he naturally sort of fell back across the bed with her she twisted her lush lips from his and gasped. "Oh, I didn't mean to *really* kiss you, you brute! Don't you understand figurative speech, damn it?"

"I figure speech pretty good, honey. Your trouble is that your refined upbringing gets in the way of what you really mean at times like these, see?"

"I see you're certainly no gentleman, Deputy Long! Kindly remove that hand from my breast, and what's that you're pressing against my thigh, and . . . Oh, wait, don't *answer* that!"

He didn't. He just kissed her some more and, after some more of the ladylike resistance they both knew was expected of her, Irene sighed and said, "It's no use. You're just too strong, and I fear I'm putty in your hands, dear."

It wasn't putty he was feeling under her thin chemise, and they both knew she hadn't really put up any struggle. For Longarm in truth was too much of a gentleman to force unwanted attentions on a weak and helpless she-male. But since she was far from being weak, thanks to the exercise she got chasing Indians all over creation, and since gals who really meant no seldom spread their thighs so when a man groped between them under a chemise, he just put the fool thing in her at full attention and paid her no mind as she bumped and ground herself against him.

He peeled the chemise off over her head and forked one of her knees over each of his elbows to get in her right. She moaned and gasped, "Darling, do it, do it, do it! Oh, I'd forgotten how good it felt. Yesss, it's happening again!"

He didn't really care how come she'd said she'd forgotten a somewhat similar experience in the past. Her past was none of his business. But naturally, as they shared a smoke afterwards, she insisted on telling him about the rascal who'd left her at the altar after using an engagement ring to have his wicked way with her.

He agreed a skunk who used such unfair tactics deserved a horse-whipping. So she giggled and said *he* hardly gave a lady a sporting chance, either. Then she asked if they could sleep some on it, as she'd had a busy day before he'd given her the business.

He chuckled and reached out to trim the lamp. The walls and her sweet naked hide next to his glowed ruby in the afterglow. He took a luxurious drag on his cheroot and mused aloud, "Funny, I don't recall lamps doing that when I was younger and more foolish."

She snuggled closer and murmured, "It's those new thorium mantles, dear. I have a lamp like that in my office. They burn hotter as well as brighter."

He started to ask her what in thunder a thorium might be, since it sounded like it belonged in someone's innards. But Longarm read the *Police Gazette* cover to cover, even the advertising, so it came back to him, and, when it did, he woke back up entirely and muttered, "Thunderation! That *could* explain a lot that otherwise makes no sense!"

As he struck a match to light the lamp again, Irene raised her sleepy face from his shoulder and asked what was wrong. He said, "Got to look at my railroad timetable. If the next train from here to Helena ain't leaving before sunrise, you can just go back to sleep."

He rolled her over out of the way, sat up, and rummaged through the pockets of his abused and crumpled frock coat until he found the timetables he liked to carry in the field. He unfolded the pages to the railroad data on this neck of the woods, found a way to make the right connections at Butte in the wee small hours, and said, "Well, there goes a perfect night I'd been planning on."

Irene rolled back over, propped herself up mighty attractively in the lamplight, and asked him what he was talking about.

He said, "We got to get up again. I don't want you here alone. I can't stay. So I'd best carry you out to the Indian camp, where you'll be safe."

"Where are you going, darling? Where *could* anyone go at this ungodly hour?"

"The territorial capital, of course. I want to be there when the offices start opening up in the morning. There's a night train due through here around two A.M. that'll take me down to Butte. From there I can get to Helena easy."

He snubbed out his smoke and reached for his socks, but Irene said, "Wait. It's nowhere's near midnight yet, and if we can't spend the whole night together . . ."

He smiled fondly down at her, nodded, and rolled back alongside her to say *adios* to this soft bed right. But as he remounted her Irene gasped, "Jesus, do you always make such sudden moves? Stop a second and tell me what's going on, aside from *this*, of course."

"Later. We got time to screw or time to talk. We ain't got time to do both. So which way do you want it, little darling?"

She didn't reply in words. She just locked her legs around the small of his back and commenced to bounce

164

her sweet rump in time with his thrusts.

He'd figured that might be the way she wanted it.

Longarm found no ticket agent on duty at the local depot after midnight. So when the two A.M. passenger train pulled in at 2:18, he just got aboard to negotiate the matter with the conductor, if he was still awake. He'd boarded in the middle of the train to make finding the rascal easier. But there was nobody up as he entered the car to his left. It was a Pullman sleeper and everybody seemed to be asleep behind the green canvas curtains on either side as he moved quietly down the aisle. Someone somewhere was snoring like a buzz-saw. Others snored more sedately as Longarm passed. The next two cars were sleepers, too. Then he came to a coach car where, though the passengers were forced to sort of sit up all night, most were dead to the world. As he passed a sleepy and not bad-looking gal, still half awake and likely finding it boring, she gave him the eye. He pretended not to see. He didn't care if she thought he was a sissy. He was going to have enough trouble staying awake all the way to Helena, thanks to that last shocking suggestion of Irene's back at the hotel.

He made his way back to the club car, where a colored barkeep was looking bored and lonesome, too. Longarm bellied up to the bar and said, "Howdy. I'd best not have anything more wilting to the brain than black coffee, if you got it."

The barkeep said he had cold coffee or tea, *iced* in fact, due to the time of the year. Longarm nodded and as the man behind the bar poured out a schooner of iced black coffee, said, "No offense, but this train don't seem to be moving and it's already running late."

The colored man said, "I just run this club car, suh.

I reckon they's picking up or putting off some mail up forward."

"Folk in Freightown sure must write lots of letters. I don't have a ticket. Reckon the conductor will get back here before it's time to get off?"

"Anyone who's still awake aboard this train will likely come this way before we reaches Butte, suh."

The train started with a jerk and Longarm took out his watch to see how late they were running. He knew he'd have an hour's layover in Butte if the railroad was running the way it was supposed to, so he was still in good shape.

He got in better shape as the train picked up speed. He had more coffee and between that and shooting the breeze with the friendly barkeep, he was wide awake when they whipped through more yards and a dimly lit town without stopping.

"Wasn't that Fort Missoula just now?" Longarm asked.

"Yessuh. We don't stop there on this run unless someone flags us. Late at night like this, nobody ever does."

Longarm sipped more coffee and mused aloud. "It sure beats all how much faster one can get about on wheels than aboard a horse. At forty miles an hour a train catches up with a hard day's ride in no time. If only there was some way to travel that fast, *off the tracks,* a man could go most anywhere and be there almost before he knew where he was going. You reckon they'll ever get them horseless carriages to work?"

"No, suh, not at no forty miles an hour. Goin' that fast off the rails would bounce folk to death before they got anywheres!"

Longarm told him he was likely right. The conductor came in and looked surprised to see him. Longarm told him who he was and what he was doing aboard the train.

The conductor said, "Oh, I know you by rep, Longarm. You can forget the ticket if you'd like to buy me a drink."

Longarm did. The conductor moved to a table across from the bar, no doubt to rest his feet. Longarm knew it would be polite to join him, but he had to stay awake, and sitting down comfortably with the lulling wheels going clickety-clack was not the way to do it. So he was standing tall at the bar when the sliding door at the end of the car opened and Beaver came in.

He blinked in surprise when he saw Longarm, of all people, there ahead of him. But he quickly recovered, smiled, and said, "Well, I never expected to see *you* here, Longarm!"

Longarm nodded soberly and said, "I know. It's about over, old son. Soon as I get to the minerals office in Helena it shouldn't take too long to dig out the last few pieces of the puzzle. You want to save me some pawing through dusty files by answering some questions here and now? I could put a good word in for you with the judge if you did."

Beaver moved to the bar and said he'd have a whiskey. Then he smiled sincerely at Longarm. "You know I'd be proud to answer any questions you put to me, Longarm," he said. "But what's this fool talk about judges?"

"So far I only got you on a charge of attempted murder," Longarm answered. "I don't know for a fact you've murdered anyone yet. I don't see who else could have gunned the Emperor Edwards back in Freighttown to keep him from talking, but we both know I can't prove it was you."

"Oh, shit, Longarm, what has this colored boy been putting in your coffee? Why the hell would I want to shoot that brakeman? I didn't even *know* the cuss."

"Do tell? Then how come you knew who we was

talking about? I said you might have gunned Edwards. I never said he was a brakeman."

Beaver tried, "Sure you did, riding up from Fort Missoula with me. You was jawing about the mean-hearted brakeman who'd locked you in that boxcar. Hell, when I heard coming across the yards that a brakeman had been shot I just put two and two together and, to tell the truth, I suspicioned it might have been *you* as shot the ornery rascal!"

Longarm nodded and said, "You're good. That'd likely hold up in court, Beaver. Now who are you going to say took a rifle shot at me from them aspens right after I turned my back on you at the army post? The colonel's lady?"

"Longarm, you're just talking mean and crazy! Why the hell would I want to bushwhack you, and if I wanted to, why didn't I do so, when you was floundering helpless in the creek that time?"

"Oh, that's easy," Longarm replied. "The folk you work for didn't want a lawman good as me poking his nose into the Indian trouble they was stirring up. So you was waiting for me at the depot, late at night, to gun me as I got off that freight. But gunning me face to face seems to make some men nervous, for some reason. So when you met your drinking buddy, the Emperor, on the loading platform, you had a safer if not better notion. You got him to lock me in. Then you rode the pony we all agreed was yours out to Kate's Crossing to rescue me and likely shoot me in the back when you had the chance. You didn't find me aboard the car. So you rode up to the Bannock camp to excuse your tracks even better than *covering* them might have. That was why you told Edwards to send the car to that particular ghost town. A man scouting Indians for the army has a mighty good excuse to ride most anywhere, don't he?"

"Longarm, you got it all wrong. I've had more than one chance to gun you in the back, and we both know you're still standing there saying awful things about me!"

"I ain't finished. After you failed at nailing me the easy way, you just two-faced me every time we met until you had a crack at me with that rifle from the aspen. When that didn't work you went back to two-facing me again, waiting for another chance. Only then you got orders *not* to gun me. So that's why you didn't, when you *did* have the drop on me for a few seconds."

"You can't have it both ways, Longarm. First you have me down as a hired assassin and then you say the crooks I'm working for decide they *likes* you?"

"I doubt they're all that fond of me. But thanks to the way you all two-faced Weeping Snakes as well, you had me going along with your game for a spell. It wouldn't have made sense to gun a U. S. deputy and draw more suspicion when you had the fool Indians acting suspicious as hell, and I was filing report after report *confirming* the Bannock were unreconstructable."

"Hell, Longarm, you saw for yourself the old medicine man was more interested in gambling than settling down. Next thing you're going to say is that I was helping him cheat, right? I sure wish you would, for I've never been as lucky at cards as *you!*"

Longarm smiled thinly and said, "I know. I slickered Weeping Snakes with a simple trick every tinhorn knows. That's how I know the old man couldn't have been cheating. He really thought he had heap big medicine. You likely told him he must have, more than once."

"You're crazy. You saw him win time after time at the tent show, and I was nowhere near him most of the time!"

"You likely went into Freighttown to send more wires to your confederates in Helena. It wasn't far, even afoot.

The way Weeping Snakes was skinning that tent show ain't no mystery. When a man in my line of work sees something impossible happening he just has to figure out what *is* possible, and the only way a mark can beat the house is to have the house let him win. It just don't work no other way."

"Oh, sure, old Duncan had a wild Indian shilling for his games of chance!"

"Not exactly. Weeping Snakes didn't know they were letting him win. He thought it was his medicine. Duncan acted proddy and put limits on how much he was allowed to win, of course. The idea was never to let the Bannock clean them out. He was just supposed to keep following them all over Robin Hood's barn as they followed the tent show farther and farther from their old hunting grounds. But, hell, why am I telling *you* all this, Beaver? You was about to tell me who's out to claim that valley the fool Indians obviously don't want, weren't you?"

Beaver pointed to his empty shot glass as he said, in the tone one might use to humor a lunatic, "Longarm, nobody wants that fool's gold in Fool's Gold Valley. There's nothing there but pipe clay with a little sand and mica in it."

"I said you was good. You're too slick to tell many fibs a man like me could catch you easy at. The thorium oxide paving that valley solid likely does look enough like plain old white clay to get you off the hook. For who would expect an army scout to know geology?"

"Now what in the hell might thorium oxide be, and where's that fool nigger with my whiskey?"

"The barkeep's under the bar, of course. He reads shifty eyes and a gun on a hip as well as me. But we know you ain't fool enough to try that way out when you fib so good, don't we? All right, to show how smart

I am, even though I know you know, thorium oxide is a sort of fancy claylike mineral you use to make expensive gas or oil lamp mantles out of. You make a thin slurry of the oxide and you dip a little cotton sack in it. You let the clay-soaked cotton weave dry stiff. Then you bake it in an oven. The cotton threads burn away to nothing, leaving you a lamp mantle of fused thorium oxide that glows almost as good as an Edison bulb when flame is applied to it. I don't know just what a ton of thorium oxide might be worth, but if it's worth *anything*, there's just tons and tons of it anywhere you want to dig in Fool's Gold Valley.

"Only now nobody will get to. I sent Irene Woodford down there with the Indians to set up a proper agency and make sure nobody does. I asked her to drop off my hired mount and some messages to other lawmen as they passed through Fort Missoula on the way. So maybe we can cut some of this bullshit if I advise you that by the time you can get to Helena your fancier confederates could well be under arrest and talking about you. Generally, when a hired killer's caught, the ones who hired him try to save their own asses by saying they never told him to go that far. You should have stuck to Indian scouting, Beaver. You ain't as smart a gun for hire as you thought."

Beaver stepped clear of the bar, still smiling. But the conductor seated behind Longarm had been following the conversation with some interest, and he must have witnessed a gunfight or more before, because he suddenly shouted, "No! God damn it! Not aboard this train!"

It was the distraction the old scout had been waiting for. He slapped leather and drew fast as hell for a man who said he had the rheumatiz.

But Longarm was faster and aimed better, so all Beaver got to blow a hole in was the rug, as Longarm doubled him over with a .44 slug in the guts. Since it was always safer to fire at least two or three times at such times, Longarm put a second round through the crown of his hat to split his skull and put him down for keeps.

Longarm stared morosely down at Beaver's body through the gunsmoke and muttered, "Well, he might have been able to fix up some loose ends for us. On the other hand, he might have confused hell out of the jury with his slick talk. So I reckon it comes out even."

The sun was up and Longarm was feeling lousy to be up by the time he got off at Helena. He'd wired the territorial law from Butte when he dropped Beaver's body off there, so a brace of Montana deputies were waiting for him at the depot.

The one in charge said, "We got a mining magnate in jail who says he's a mighty important cuss, Longarm. I sure hope you can prove your case agin him."

Longarm yawned. "So far I don't even know the son of a bitching claim jumper's name. How come you arrested him so soon? I only wired I suspicioned anyone claiming mineral rights in Fool's Gold Valley recent was to stay in town until I could get here."

"You ain't the only smart bastard who packs a badge, Longarm," the Montana lawman said. "The rascal's name is Epworth, and he's got a record as long as you're tall. He mostly goes in for selling blue-sky mining stock. But on occasion, when there's really something in the ground to be dug, he forms a legitimate company to dig some and then sell out. So he left a mighty broad paper trail for us to look at when we got the mining office to open early. Epworth is on file as having bought out the original prospecting claims in Fool's Gold Valley for little more

172

than train fare home for them greenhorns. He's been fighting the BIA by way of the Land Office ever since to get the Bannock's prior claim on the land set aside so's he can dig for fool's gold."

The other Montana lawman chuckled and said, "That's what he said when we arrested him as he was having breakfast. He said it was a free country and that if nobody else wanted to dig for mica he had a right to. He must have forgotten that just the other day he filed for papers incorporating him as the Montana Thorium Trust, Inc."

"Yeah," Longarm said, "he must have figured he'd better, once he had the Indians so far out of that valley the army was bound to want to pin 'em down *any* old place, if they didn't want to settle where the BIA suggested. I'd better talk to him before I fall asleep."

They led him out front, where, praise the Lord, they'd thought to provide an open carriage. They all piled in and it was only a short drive to the territorial holding cages. Longarm was still yawning a lot as they went into the red-brick building and asked the desk sergeant to run the rascal out for them.

As the Montana lawmen watched with interest, Longarm sat the puffed-up-looking, middle-aged T. K. Epworth at a table in the side room they used for such conversations. Longarm remained standing. He yawned and said, "I ain't up to a tedious discussion of your sins, Epworth. We got you cold on murder in the first, and you're so ugly I don't care if they hang you right side up or by the heels. But since I'm willing to agree you might not have known the murdered man personally enough to matter, I'll tell you what I'm going to let you do. I'm going to let you plead to criminal conspiracy. You just confess all the other dirty deeds you done and we'll drop the murder charge, hear?"

173

The prisoner stared up thunderstruck and shouted loudly, "It's a lie! It's a frame-up! I've never murdered anybody, and you know it!"

Longarm yawned again and said, "You ordered Beaver Ashton to murder me. When that didn't work, he murdered another rascal who might have been able to tell me Beaver's name or at least describe him. Beaver was there in town the night I got off the train, and . . . Why am I telling everybody things they already know? I'd best stick to things you might *not* know yet, since night letters are often delivered after the time this morning you were arrested. Beaver made a full confession down in Butte as he lay dying in the cold gray dawn. He was dying because I shot him before he could shoot me, on your direct orders. That puts the blood on your hands, Epworth."

"No! It ain't true! I told Beaver to ease off and let you be, God damn it! If he tried to gun you it was his own notion, not mine!"

Then Epworth saw the way the Montana lawmen were looking at one another and said, "All right. I'll admit I hired an old army scout who knows the area to keep an eye on things there until I could file a claim on . . . sure, why not, some fairly valuable mineral deposits. Is it my fault nobody else can tell thorium oxide from common clay, or that not even the Indians want the fool place?"

Longarm said, "It sure is. Weeping Snakes was born in that valley. It's well wooded and watered, and for once the army and the BIA was willing to leave Indians in peace on their own hunting ground. But you got your sidekick, Salty Sam Simmons, to pay off another con man running a tent show to sucker the Indians out of the valley and off the thorium oxide flats you wanted. Oh, I forgot to tell you, Salty Sam's confessed, too. They're holding him for us in Fort Missoula."

Epworth groaned. "Oh, Jesus, what did he go back *there* for? He was supposed to be in *Superior* by now!"

Longarm yawned and stretched. "I'm sure if one of you boys would be kind enough to fetch a pencil and paper, Mr. Epworth would be proud to clear this matter up for us now."

The junior deputy said, "I'll get a pen and ink if it's all the same with you, Longarm. I hope you understand who's got the jurisdiction here?"

"Sure. Montana can have him, stuffed, for all I care. My job was to neaten up the Indian situation for the BIA. My boss won't care who does the paperwork."

The deputy was soon back with proper writing material and the ringleader was writing properly before Longarm could change his mind. A lawman who had you cold and just stood there fighting to stay awake tended to make a man with a guilty conscience sweat.

When Epworth had signed away his next few years of freedom and been taken back to his holding cell, Longarm told the Montana lawmen they could find him at the nearest hotel, as he was too tired to walk a step farther than he had to. As they walked out front with him, one chuckled and asked, "'Fess up, Longarm. How much of that act you just put on in there was pure bluff, and how much was true?"

"I fibbed a mite, I'll allow," Longarm said. "But how was *he* to know what Beaver Ashton might or might not have said going down with a bullet in his head, or that nobody else has been arrested?"

"Jesus Christ! You mean Salty Sam *wasn't* picked up in Fort Missoula?"

"Not hardly. You just heard him say the bastard was in Superior. I'll wire Superior about it later, after I get my head clear. I reckon we ought to at least get a confirming statement from Salty Sam. They'll generally sign away a partner to keep from going to jail with him, and Salty Sam Simmons ain't nothing but a piss-ant when nobody's funding him."

"What about the crooks running that tent show, Long-arm?"

"Nobody can stop crooks from running tent shows as long as a sucker's getting born every minute, boys. Old Duncan's already been punished as much as the law allows. Last night he let Weeping Snakes take him for a heap of cash he'll never see again, now that the gent paying him to let the Indian win is out of business. Can I go now? It ain't seemly for a gent as delicate-natured as me to sleep on a sidewalk in broad day. But I sure gotta sleep *somewhere* right now."

# Chapter 15

Longarm had expected to sleep forever once he hit that hotel bed all by himself. But he woke up before sundown hungry as a wolf and feeling otherwise just fine. So he got up, got cleaned and shaved, and got out of there to get some supper.

He found a beanery serving hot coffee and chile con carne a mite cooler than he liked it. He topped it off with apple pie and headed for the Western Union to tell Billy Vail how smart he was and that he'd be catching the next train south to Denver. The papers were already out on the stands in Helena, headlining what an awful person T. K. Epworth was and reminding others he'd bilked in the past that he was pinned down where process servers could get at him for a change. So, after he got through making small rocks out of big ones for Montana, he figured to find other judges and juries waiting in line for him.

Longarm found a wire waiting for him at the telegraph

office. Vail had read the afternoon papers, too, but he said wild guesses just weren't good enough for the final report they had to file. So Longarm was to go down to Fool's Gold Valley, scoop up at least a few ounces of the mysterious clay, and let a government chemist say for sure if there was a trace of thorium oxide in it or not.

Longarm wired that he sure would. He didn't think old Billy needed to know he hadn't had enough of Irene yet.

Then he trudged over to the depot, taking out his railroad timetable as he went to read it on the fly. For once they were running a railroad right, and in no time at all he was on his way to Butte. Butte wasn't where he was going, but he had to change there and, damn it to hell, the gal he got to talking to in the club car had to stay on the infernal train when they arrived only an hour or so later. So the longer switchback up to Fort Missoula felt even more tedious than it might have.

He got off at last. It was dark now, but still early, and a Saturday night as well. So the main street was crowded, and the hotel he'd stayed at before with Jemima was overflowing. They told him they could fix him up a pallet on a pool table, once the poolroom closed, but he said he'd rather ride at night than sleep on a pool table, so he headed for the livery.

As he got there, one of the officers from the military post was just leaving his own mount there. He hailed Longarm and said, "We just heard about Beaver. Who ever would have thought it?"

"Well, he had to slip up some before *I* did, Captain. Say, could you do me a favor? I still have to settle with your colonel for the loss of an army mount, and I may as well pay him for the saddle I hope the BIA left here for me as well, so..."

"Forget it," the captain said with a grin. "We can always write it off as wastage, and we owe you for the way you got the army off the hook when you filed your report on Beaver."

"Wouldn't have been fair to accuse the army of being in on a crooked scheme they knew nothing about, Captain. We were way off the military reserve when he made his move, in any case. So it's all over."

The captain nodded, but said, "All but the part about those two missing carnival girls. If the Indians didn't kidnap them, who do you suppose did? The gang Beaver was working with?"

"Not hardly. For one thing, it was just a crooked would-be mining magnate, not a real gang. And, for another, none of the gents at all involved in the case would have had any use for a couple of sassy bawds." He checked his watch. "Hell, I figure to get to Fool's Gold Valley late no matter what. So let's see if we can scout up the missing white captives, Captain."

"Swell. I'll get my horse back."

"Don't. They ain't far enough out in Indian territory for us to need horses, if I'm right. A man has to guess right *once* in a while."

This time he was. The young officer followed him with growing uneasiness as he saw where Longarm was leading him. At the bottom of the whorehouse steps he said, "Longarm, I can't go into a place like this in dress uniform!"

"Sure you can," Longarm said. "I may need your imposing blue duds to back my play. Whores hardly ever tell anyone the truth unless they think they have to."

He led the reluctant officer into the house of ill repute and told the maid who opened the door for them to fetch the madam on the double.

She did. The fat, ugly woman in the too-tight pretty gown smiled at them, cast her gaze at the captain's dress blues, and said, "My, my, this is a pleasant surprise."

"No, it ain't," Longarm said, "We're here on official business as agents of the U. S. Government."

"Oh, my God! Since when has screwing become a federal offense?"

Longarm said, "You got two new girls working here. We can work it two ways. You can trot 'em out or you can just tell us the truth."

"The truth about Tillie and Sunshine Sal? Hell, what can I tell you about either, once we're all agreed they're whores!"

Longarm said, "I've been in enough places like this to know the house rules, ma'am. Working whores ain't allowed to level with the customers even if they want to. But it ain't professional for a whore to hold anything back on her madam."

"That's true enough, but I assure you all I can tell you about them is that they're young and enthusiastic and—"

"And if you don't cut out this bullshit the captain here can have this place declared off limits to soldiers, and you'll damn near starve between pay nights for the cowhands!" Longarm cut in. "I just come from Freighttown where the whores is starving. So that was likely why they come down *here* to work when they run off from the tent show the other night, right?"

The madam hesitated.

He said, "We ain't interested in the booth tills they emptied as they saw a way to light out in the confusion of a Hey Rube. Their old boss might not even know they helped themselves to some hard-earned cash and came down here to earn more, in a more relaxed position. We

180

don't want to *arrest* 'em. We just want 'em off the books as captives of wild Indians. So, true or false—ain't Tillie really named Edith, and ain't the one called Sunshine Sal a blonde named Joy?"

The madam laughed sheepishly and said, "Hell, it ain't no skin off my personal ass. They said they'd rather work lying down than on their poor, aching feet and not getting a fair share of the take. As to whether they stole any back wages they thought they had coming, you'll have to take it up with them. I told them they were on their own if they were in trouble with the law. I run a whorehouse, not a hideout!"

Longarm turned to the young officer. "You heard all you need to know, Captain?"

The other man said, "Hell, yes! The outfit will get a feather in its cap for clearing up the matter entirely for the War Department's files! I don't see why the army should be interested in the internal affairs of a traveling tent show. Could we get out of here before some enlisted men come in or out? I have enough sniggering in the ranks to deal with as it is!"

Longarm nodded, thanked the madam for her time, and the two men left together. Out on the street the captain asked Longarm what he was drinking.

Longarm said, "I thank you for the invite. But I got a long ride ahead of me tonight. So let's just shake on it and I'll be on my way."

They did, and Longarm turned away to stride toward the livery as the captain stared after him fondly, reaching in his tunic for a cigar. He thought, grinned, then took out two as he realized a good cigar was as good as a drink to say thanks with. But Longarm's long legs had already taken him way down the walk by then and so, not wanting to yoo-hoo after him like a she-male, the

181

young officer went after him at the same pace, knowing Longarm would have to slow down when he got to the livery just down the street.

Naturally, Longarm had no idea he was being followed by anyone, so he was startled enough to spin around and drop to one knee when he heard someone yell, "Longarm! *Duck!*"

It had been a mighty good suggestion, Longarm knew, when gun muzzles flashed in the gloom he'd just passed through and at least one round passed over his head too close for comfort. He'd drawn his own gun as he spun and ducked, of course, but it wasn't too clear who he should be shooting at just now. He spied the familiar blue uniform of the captain coming his way, his own service revolver out but not aiming at him. Between them a dark form lay face down on the boardwalk, with a Remington .38 lying harmless but still smoking near one outstretched hand.

As Longarm got to the smaller-than-expected gunslinger and bent to turn him over, the captain ran up and gasped, "He was about to shoot you in the back! He let you walk past him and then stepped out of that dark doorway over there with his gun already aimed! Thank God I had two cigars!"

Longarm thought that was a mighty odd thing to say at a time like this, but lots of men said dumb things when they were rattled by a shooting. It was more important to find out who the hell was still shooting at him. Who could be left?

He rolled the shabbily dressed stranger over. It was Jemima.

Longarm gasped and said, "Aw, hell, God, that wasn't fair!"

The girl the captain had shot in the back to keep her

from doing the same to Longarm opened her eyes and murmured, "Damn you, Custis, you done me dirty, just like you done my *daddy* dirty!"

The captain gasped. "Oh, my God, I've shot a woman!"

Longarm told him to hush as he felt Jemima for bullet holes while he asked her gently, "What are you talking about, honey? I never even met your father. He wasn't here when we arrived at the army post, remember?"

"You kilt him in Denver," Jemima insisted. "I found out when I got off the train down there. It was in all the papers, with my poor daddy's picture. I don't know why he was going around saying his name was Bannerman when everyone knows it was really Nolan. But that don't matter. What matters is that you *kilt my daddy,* the one true father I ever had, and now I've got to kill you."

Longarm found where she'd been hit, bad, and looked up bleakly to tell the captain, "Go find a doctor, fast!"

But as the gunplay had attracted the usual small-town attention and some townees were already starting to gather, one do-gooder in the bunch shouted that he'd go get the doc. It was just as well. The officer who had shot Jemima was just standing there staring down at her, looking shocked. Longarm said gently, "I know how you feel. I thank you anyway. I reckon there may be something to the notion of impulsive natures running in families. I never killed her fool father. But you just saw how she took after him when it came to flying off the handle for dumb reasons."

Jemima coughed. "I *had* my reasons, damn you! You kilt my daddy and then you covered up so's you could have your wicked way with me and, oh, I think you're so mean I don't ever intend to speak to you again!"

She must have meant it, for by the time a portly gent with a black bag got there, she was dead. Longarm got wearily to his feet as the doctor went to work on the pathetic little girl anyway, as if there was anything medical science could do for her now. He took the revolver from the officer's limp hand and put it in its army holster for him. Then he said, "I'll take you up on that drink now. We're going to be stuck here a spell, answering questions and signing statements for the local law. Let me do most of the talking. I've had more experience with such matters."

The captain muttered numbly, "It was a girl, a pretty girl! I've never shot a white person before and to think when I did it had to be a *girl!*"

"Let's go have that drink. Maybe we'd best have more than one. I'm feeling sort of sick about it, too, for it was more my fault than yourn she felt the way she did about me."

So the coroner found them in the saloon, drinking pretty good, and allowed he'd have some redeye too, as Longarm explained how the late Logan Bannerman's daughter had taken after her father a mite even though he'd spent most of her girlhood in prison, writing home that he was an army scout to explain the distance between them.

The coroner didn't make much of a fuss about what had happened. Well before midnight it had all been settled and Longarm was on his way south in the moonlight. He still felt drained by the needless tragedy, for Jemima had been a sweet little thing when she wasn't trying to follow in her father's footsteps. But she had, and he had to allow the world was doubtless a mite safer for sensible folk with both father and daughter out of it. So he told himself to forget it and told his mount to move faster. At the rate they were going, it would be well after sunrise by the time they got to Fool's Gold Valley, or Kitlaztlan, to give it its proper and now more likely permanent name.

The livery horse tried, but when it stumbled over a log across the trail in the dark and nearly threw him, Longarm checked the reins gently and muttered, "Oh, hell, there's no real hurry. I reckon we can talk old Irene into serving us breakfast in bed no matter *how* late in the morning we get there."